Ted & Paul

The Battle for Sleepy Hollow

Keith Godwin

DEDICATION

This book is dedicated to two of my former pupils.

Kelly East (Kelly Jarrett when she was my pupil back in 1988), has been the driving force behind this book and without her Ted & Paul would never have been published.

I have also been very fortunate to have another past pupil involved, artist Patrick J Killian who designed the front cover.

My sincere and grateful thanks go to both of them.

CONTENTS

FOREWORD

This is the first of a number of stories (7 in total) about the adventures, or perhaps I should say misadventures of two brothers, Ted & Paul Thomas.

In this first story, they come to the rescue of Mrs. Muldoon, an old lady who lives in a house in the woods which is being threatened with demolition by the local council to make way for a new by-pass round their village.

It tells how they battle to defend Sleepy Hollow and stop the council from evicting their new friend and her strange collection of pets.

BACKGROUND

I was a teacher at Cwmcarn Primary School in the beautiful Welsh Valleys for 36 years. I taught pupils from 1972 to 2008. During my early years there, I started telling my class stories that I had written about 'Ted & Paul.'

The stories came in handy time and time again as the children would always know that if they weren't on their best behavior, I would not be reading them pages from my Ted & Paul stories at the end of the school day.

Over the years, I ended up writing seven stories altogether, enough to last the whole of the school year. Throughout the 36 years I taught at Cwmcarn Primary, I must have read them to well over a thousand of my pupils.

Whenever I meet any of those pupils today, they always ask the same question, "When are you going to publish your Ted & Paul stories Sir?" They've had a long wait, but now, thanks to Kelly they are at last being published.

My former pupils at Cwmcarn may have forgotten much of what I taught them, but they certainly have not forgotten the Ted & Paul stories.

I hope they will get as much enjoyment reading them now, as they did when they first heard me reading them in my class all those years ago.

Ted & Paul – The Battle for Sleepy Hollow was originally written in August 1976. 45 Years later, it has finally been published!

CHAPTER 1

THE BATTLE FOR SLEEPY HOLLOW

This is the story of two brothers: Edward, better known as Ted, and his brother, Paul. They live in a terraced house in one of the valleys of South Wales. Their father is employed by a big engineering firm while their mother spends all of her time looking after her husband and two sons. Ted is the older of the two brothers by almost a year. He is nearly ten while his brother, Paul, is nine. They both go to the local junior school and are in the same class. Of the two boys, Paul is the better behaved and rarely gets into trouble. Ted, on the other hand, is always getting himself into trouble. He doesn't mean to - it just seems to happen to him.

Our story starts the day before the Easter holidays were due to begin. The boys had gone to school and the day had started as it usually did. Lessons were the same with their teacher, Miss Hughes, keeping them hard at work and making sure that Ted did not make a nuisance of himself in class. After playtime when the children had come in from the playground and settled down, Miss Hughes spoke to the class.

"Children, as you know, at four o'clock you start two weeks holiday."
"Great." muttered Ted. "It will be good to get away from school and teachers."

Unfortunately, Miss Hughes heard him.

"Ted, will you keep quiet."
"Sorry Miss." apologised Ted.
"To continue with what I was saying." said Miss Hughes. "this holiday I want you to do some work for me."
"But Miss," began Ted, "it's our holiday."
"Just let me finish, will you Ted?"
"Sorry Miss." apologised Ted again.

Miss Hughes continued:

"The work I want you to do is a project on the village. During the holiday, I want you to find out something interesting about the village. When you come back after the holidays you can tell the class what you have found out and there will be a prize for the best one."

At the mention of the word 'prize', the children began to pay more attention. None of them were looking forward to doing schoolwork during the holidays but if there was a prize, that was a different matter.

"What'll the prize be Miss?" asked Paul.
"Oh, it'll be a mystery prize, you'll have to wait until after the holidays to find out what it is." Miss Hughes told him.
"What kind of things can we do for this project, Miss?" asked Peter.
"I'll give you some ideas," said Miss Hughes, "but you can choose an idea of your own if you wish."

The class listened while their teacher gave them some ideas:

"You could find out about coal mining and the colliery which used to be in the village." suggested Miss Hughes.
"Peter, you're interested in trains, you might like to find out about the railway and when the trains ran through the village. Someone might like to find out about roads and transport, that's very topical with the new by-pass being built around the village. Someone might like to find out about the buildings in the village. That's just a few suggestions. I'm sure you could think of many more."
When the bell went for dinner time Miss Hughes

dismissed the class and they went to the canteen for their meal. In the playground after lunch, Ted, Paul and their friend, Peter, were talking about the mystery prize for the best project. Ted noticed some boys from Class 13 coming towards them. The boys were members of the village gang. Ted, Paul, and Peter were not in the gang!

"Hi John." said Ted as they came over. "What do you want?"
"Nothing," John replied, "Just me and the gang were wondering if you would like to join."
"What? Join the Grizzly Gang?" asked Ted excitedly.
"That's what I said," replied John. "The gang and I think you three would make good gang members. What do you say?"

Ted and Peter were all for joining the gang there and then, but Paul wasn't so sure. Before either Ted or Peter could accept the offer, he spoke to John.
"It's good of you to offer us the chance of joining the gang." said Paul. "Can we have some time to think it over?"
"Sure." said John, "We're having a gang meeting at the Swing Tree in the wood tomorrow at ten

o'clock. If you want to join, be there. If you're not there we'll know you're too scared to become members."

"I thought the council had started knocking the wood down to make way for the new by-pass," said Peter.

"They've got the equipment there, but they haven't begun yet." answered John.

"See you tomorrow morning." said Ted, who was keen to become a member of the gang.

The bell went for the afternoon and the children all trooped into the building. There was no chance to discuss the offer of becoming members of the Grizzly Gang until after school. That afternoon when the bell went at four o'clock. Ted, Paul, and Peter made their way to the park to talk about John's offer.

"I think we should join the gang." announced Ted sitting down on one of the swings.

"So do I." agreed Peter. "It would be great being a member of the Grizzly Gang."

"Why do you think we should join?" asked Paul.

"Because it's the best gang in the village," said Ted keenly.

"Yes," said Peter, "everyone knows the Grizzly Gang."

"And why does everyone know the Grizzly Gang?" asked Paul.

Ted and Peter were silent. They knew only too well why everyone knew the Grizzly Gang.

"I'll tell you why," continued Paul. "They're so well-known because they're always getting into some sort of trouble."

Ted and Peter were forced to agree, the Grizzly Gang were always getting into trouble in the village.

"Remember when they went collecting Penny for the Guy?" asked Paul.
"Yes" giggled Ted. "They tied up Terry Jones in a push-chair, put a mask on his face and used him for the Guy."
"Terry didn't think it was very funny, neither did his mother who reported the gang to the police," said Paul.
"They made a lot of money though." pointed out Ted.
"And we needn't get mixed up in anything like that." added Peter.
"That's right." agreed Ted. "I vote we join the gang. Peter and I are going to join even if you

don't."

This presented Paul with a problem. He didn't really want to join the gang because he knew they would end up getting in some sort of trouble, especially Ted. If he didn't join the gang there was no telling what mischief Ted would get into. If he did join, at least he could keep an eye on his brother and try and keep him out of trouble. Reluctantly, he decided to join the gang.

"All right." he announced. "I'll join the gang with you."
"Great" said Ted, "It wouldn't be the same if we joined and you didn't."
"I'd better be getting home." said Peter.
"O.K" said Ted, "Call for us at half-past nine tomorrow and we'll go to the Swing Tree together."

Peter ran off home and Ted and Paul walked home together.
"I can't wait for tomorrow morning." said Ted excitedly.

CHAPTER 2

THE GRIZZLY GANG

The next morning was Saturday. Ted was awake at half-past eight. Ten minutes later he was washed and dressed and charging down the stairs. He burst into the kitchen. His father glared at him.

"I do wish you would not come down the stairs like a runaway elephant." snapped Mr. Thomas.
"Sorry Dad, I forgot." apologised Ted.

His father was always complaining about the way he charged down the stairs. Ted meant to walk but he always forgot and got into trouble with his Dad.

"What are you doing up this early?" asked his mother.
"Thought I'd get up early for a change" replied Ted.
"That certainly is a change." said his father.
"You've never been up this early on a Saturday."
"Usually, I can't get him out of bed in the mornings." commented his mother.
"So, what's so special about today?" asked his

father.

"Nothing special Dad," said Ted. "Just thought as it was the first day of the holidays I'd get up and enjoy it."

Mr. Thomas looked at his son suspiciously. It was strange for him to be up this early. Something was going on and he wished he had time to find out what it was. Unfortunately, he was running late for work and had to leave. He got up from the table, collected his briefcase and kissed his wife goodbye. He looked over to Ted.

"Try and stay out of trouble." he warned his son.
"Who, me?" said Ted.
"Yes, you!" said Mr. Thomas and left for work.
"Bloomin' cheek." said Ted. "Anyone would think that I was always getting into trouble."
"Well, you do seem to get into more trouble than anyone else." pointed out his mother.
"And where's that brother of yours?" she asked.
"Still snoring away in bed, I expect." said Ted.
"Well, you'd better go and get him up." said Mrs. Thomas. "If he wants breakfast this morning, he'd better be down here in ten minutes, or he'll go hungry."

Ted left the kitchen and went upstairs. This time

he walked, but unfortunately his father was not there to see it.

Crossing the landing, he pushed open the bedroom door. There was no sign of Paul, just a big lump under the blankets which Ted knew was his sleeping brother. He walked over to the bed.

"Rise and shine." he yelled.

There was no movement from beneath the pile of blankets.

"Come on, Paul." said Ted, giving his brother a prod.

"Gerrroff!" came the mumbled reply from under the bedclothes.

"It's time to get up." insisted Ted, pulling the blankets off his brother.

Paul immediately pulled the blankets back over himself.

"It's nine o'clock." said Ted. "Mam says if you don't get up now you won't be getting any breakfast."

Grumbling and complaining, Paul sat up in bed and gave a huge yawn. He got out of bed and stretched. He had decided he would rather be up early and have breakfast than get up late and miss it. Already the smell of cooking bacon was wafting upstairs and was making him feel very hungry. He made his way to the bathroom while Ted charged back down the stairs into the kitchen.

"Ted." said his mother, "What did your father say about coming down the stairs?"
"Sorry Mam, I forgot." said Ted.

Five minutes later both boys were sitting at the kitchen table tucking into their breakfasts.

"What are you going to do today?" asked their mother.
"Mumph, gurgle, gurgle, gulp." answered Ted with a mouthful of food.
"What did he say?" Mrs. Thomas asked her other son.
"I think he said 'mumph, gurgle, gurgle, gulp'." repeated Paul.
"Oh, very funny." said his mother, not at all amused. "Ted, how many times have you been told not to speak with your mouth full."
"Sorry Mam." said Ted. "We're meeting Peter and we're going to find out about the village for a

school project."

"That sounds very interesting." said his mother. "And it should keep you out of trouble."

"We'll be gone for most of the day." added Ted.

"But we will be back for tea."

"That suits me." said Mrs. Thomas.

The front doorbell rang.

"That will be Peter." explained Paul. "We told him to call for us."

"Off you go then." said his mother. "And make sure you behave yourselves."

"We always do Mam." said Ted, leaving before his mother could contradict him.

The three boys set off down the road talking amongst themselves as they went. At the end of the street, they crossed the road which ran through the village and turned down School Lane, passing their school on the way to the wood.

The Swing Tree where they were to meet the gang was in the middle of the wood and got its name from the rope that hung from one of the branches. It was a favourite spot with the children, but since the gang has started using it as their meeting place, many of the children stayed well away from it. The last time Ted had been there he had fallen off the swing into a muddy puddle and got his clothes in a dreadful state, for which he had got into big trouble with his parents.

As they approached the meeting place, they could see that the gang was already there. Ted could see John, the leader of the gang, with the other members, David, Gary, Gwyn, and Richard who were sitting under the tree, while Vincent was hanging on the rope being pushed by Tony. They watched as the three boys walked over to join them.

"Glad you could make it," said John. "I think you know everyone here, and they know you."

The boys nodded to each other. Paul was wondering what they would have to do to become members of the gang. He was sure there would be some sort of test they would have to pass before being accepted. He was not wrong, as he soon found out.

"Before you join the gang, you have to undergo a small test." John informed the three boys.

"What sort of test?" asked Paul suspiciously.

"A test to see if you are brave enough to be called a member of the Grizzly Gang." said Gary.

"And just what do we have to do to prove we are brave enough?" asked Peter, a little worried at the mention of the test.

"It's quite an easy test." said John with a smile on his face. "You have to go to Sleepy Hollow."

There was silence. The three boys looked at each other and for several moments no one spoke.

Sleepy Hollow is the name of a large old house to be found in the woods. It belonged to an old lady called Mrs. Muldoon, who lived in the house alone, except for a selection of animals she kept as pets. The house was in a poor state of repair and very spooky. Most of the children in the village believed it was haunted and some even believed Mrs. Muldoon was a witch. Mrs. Muldoon lived a lonely life some of the children teased and made fun of her. As a result of this she didn't like children and whenever she saw any hanging about her house, she would shout at them and chase them away. It was to her house that Ted, Paul, and Peter had to go to prove they were brave enough to become members of the gang. They were rather worried about this, but they were not going to let the gang know they were frightened.

"I don't think they want to go." sniggered Gary.
"Perhaps they're scared." added David.
"We're not scared of anything." snapped Ted defiantly.
"Not afraid of Mad Mrs. Muldoon?" asked Gwyn.
"She's…. she's….she's not mad….is she?" asked a rather worried Peter.
"People say she can turn children into animals." said John, trying hard not to smile.
"Or eats them for dinner." added Vincent.
"Don't be silly." said Paul. "You're only trying to scare us."
"Oh, you'll go then?" asked John.
"Yes, we'll go," said Ted, before Paul or Peter could stop him.
"Oh, there's one small thing I forgot to mention." added John.
"What's that?" asked Peter.
"You have to go there at night." John told them.
"At night?" gulped Peter.
"But it will be dark."
"It usually is at night." laughed Tony.
"That's what makes it a real test." announced John. "Do you want to back out?"

"Certainly not." said Ted who did really but wasn't going to admit it.

"What time does the test start?"

"Be back here at half-past seven this evening if you're brave enough." he told them.

"We'll be here," said Ted.

The gang began to leave, laughing as they went. Ted, Paul, and Peter watched them go. The boys were no longer so keen to become members of the Grizzly Gang now that they knew what they had to do to become members. They sat down under the Swing Tree.

"What do you think?" Paul asked the other two.

"Think about what?" asked his brother.

"About coming back here tonight of course." said Paul.

"We've got to come back here tonight, or we won't be made members of the gang." pointed out Ted.

"I don't think I want to become a member of the gang anymore." said Peter.

"You can't back out now or they'll call you a chicken," said Ted.

"I can think of worse things." replied Peter. "Like going to Sleepy Hollow tonight."

"I'm afraid Ted's right, Peter." said Paul. "If we back out now, they'll take great enjoyment telling everyone in school we were scared. They'll make our lives a misery."

"Besides," said Ted trying to reassure Peter. "I don't think we will come to any harm."

"But what if she turns us into animals?" asked Peter.

"Well, if she does, then I'll ask her to change me into a lion." laughed Ted.

"And I'll ask her to turn me into a horse." added Paul, joining in the fun.

"What about you Pete?" asked Ted. "What would you like her to turn you into?"

"I'd prefer to stay as I am." replied Peter. "But if I'm going to be turned into something I'd like to be changed into a bird so I could fly."

"Come on." said Ted "Let's go and have a game of football in the park."

"I've got to do some shopping for my mother." said Peter. "But I'll walk with you as far as the shops."

They left the Swing Tree and made their way back through the woods to the village. In the main street Peter left them, arranging to call for them at seven o'clock. Ted and Paul went to the park and joined some of their friends in a game of football, though their minds were not on the game. They were thinking of what was going to happen that evening when they would undergo their test to become members of the Grizzly Gang.

CHAPTER 3

SLEEPY HOLLOW

At seven o'clock that evening the front doorbell rang and Mr. Thomas went to answer it. He let Peter in and came back into the front room with him.

"We're just going out for a bit." announced Ted standing up.
"It's a bit late to be going out, isn't it?" asked his father.
"We won't be long Dad." promised Paul.
"Make sure you're back by nine o'clock." said his father.
"O.K." said Ted. "We will be."
"You'd better be." warned his mother coming into the room. "Or you'll get no supper."

The boys left the house and hurried down the street, crossed the main road, went down School Lane and entered the wood. It was beginning to get dark and walking through the trees made it seem even darker. Peter shivered; he was not at all looking forward to this evening. Mind you, Ted and Paul were not exactly over the moon about it either. They walked towards the Swing

19

Tree.

When they arrived, they found the members of the gang waiting for them.

"I didn't think you would come." sneered John.
"Well, you thought wrong, didn't you." said Ted.
"Are you ready to start the test?" asked Tony.
"Yes." answered the three boys together.
"Right. Off you go then." said John.
"One question." said Paul.
"What is it?" asked Vincent.
"How are you going to check, to make sure we go?" asked Paul.
"Oh, we'll be watching from a safe distance." chuckled John. "Any other questions?"

There were no more questions and without further ado, Ted, Paul, and Peter set off through the woods towards Sleepy Hollow. The gang sat and watched them go. When the three boys had disappeared from sight, the gang began laughing at the trick they had played on Ted, Paul, and Peter. They made their way back through the woods to the village. They had no intention of following the boys. They were going home. There was no way they would go to Sleepy Hollow. What if Mrs. Muldoon could turn children into animals? They were not going to risk that.

Meanwhile, Ted, Paul and Peter had reached the garden wall that ran round Sleepy Hollow. It was quite dark now and there was no moon. The wall was very high and impossible to climb without a ladder.

"Let's see if we can find a gate." suggested Ted.

They began walking outside the wall. The front gate they found was locked. They could see the bolt that locked it on the other side of the gate but could not reach it.

"If we can't get in, we can't complete the test." said Peter, rather relieved that they could not open the gate.

"It does look as though Peter is right." agreed Paul.

"We can't give up." announced Ted. "We'll get over the wall."

"And just how do you intend to do that?" asked his brother.

"Pole-vault over it?"

"I've an idea." said Ted.

"I was afraid you would." said Paul.

"If you stood on my shoulders, you should be able to reach the top of the wall and lower yourself down the other side."

"I've an even better idea." said Paul. "You stand on my shoulders, and you go over the wall!"

"O.K by me." agreed Ted.

"I don't fancy climbing over that wall." said Peter.

"You won't have to Pete." said Ted. "Once I get down the other side, I'm sure I'll be able to unbolt the gate and let you and Paul in."

Paul knelt down and Ted climbed onto his shoulders. Paul began to stand with his brother on his shoulders, hands against the wall to stop them losing their balance. It wasn't easy. Ted wasn't exactly a lightweight. Unfortunately, he still could not reach the top of the wall.

"If I were to stand on his head, I should be able to reach." thought Ted.

"What are you doing?" demanded Paul, feeling his brothers shoe on the top of his head.

Ted didn't answer, as grabbing the top of the wall he pulled himself up and sat on it looking down at the other two below him.

"Why did you do that?" asked Paul angrily.

"I used my head to solve the problem." replied

Ted.

"You did not." said Paul rubbing his head.

"You used my head to solve the problem."

"It's pretty high up here." Ted told them.

"Lower yourself down quietly." called up Paul.

"Right." called back Ted.

Ted began to lower himself and soon he was hanging from the top of the wall by his fingertips. He was unable to feel the ground with his feet so he decided he would have to drop the rest of the way and hope for a soft landing. He let go and dropped.

"Arrrrgghhhh!" came the yell from the far side of the wall.

"Be quiet." whispered Paul.

"What's happened?" asked Peter anxiously.

"You try keeping quiet if you landed in a pile of nettles." came Ted's voice from the other side.

Paul and Peter tried hard not to laugh.

"Hurry up and open the gate." called Paul.

Grumbling to himself, Ted made his way along the inside of the wall towards the garden gate while Paul and Peter made their way along the outside of the wall. Ted reached the gate and tried to unbolt it. The bolt would not move.

"The bolt is stuck." he told the other two waiting on the other side of the gate.
"Try and find a stone to hit it with." suggested Paul.
"Good idea." called back Ted.

He went off to find a stone and came back with one a minute later. He struck the bolt with it. A loud CLANG echoed round the garden.

"Sshhh!" hissed Paul. "Do it quietly!"
"Don't be daft." hissed back Ted. "How can you hit a metal bolt with a stone quietly?"
"Try it." said Paul.
"No need to." replied Ted, "It's done the trick, the bolt has moved."

Peter and Paul pushed the gate and it swung open, squeaking on its hinges.

"Needs oiling." Ted commented.
"Come on." said Paul. "Let's get on with it. It's almost too dark to see."
"I wish we'd brought a torch." said Ted.
"Keep close together, we don't want to get separated." warned Peter.

They crept down the path towards the dark shape that was Sleepy Hollow. Even though Peter had warned about getting separated, they managed to do just that. Ted went straight down the path towards the house, Paul took the path to the left and Peter took the path to the right. It was a couple of minutes before they realised they were no longer together.

Inside the house, Mrs. Muldoon was about to let her pets out into the garden for a run before she locked up for the night and went to bed. She did this every evening. She treated her animals like children, had given each of them a name and they lived in comfort in the old house with her.

"Now I don't want you to be long tonight." she addressed her pets. "I'm rather tired and want to get to bed. Ten minutes only."

The animals looked at her.

"Off you go Dilys." said Mrs. Muldoon to her pet donkey and Dilys trotted out of the house into the garden.

"Off you slither Samantha." said Mrs. Muldoon to her pet snake, and off Samantha slithered down the steps into the darkness.

"You next Henry and Henrietta." said Mrs. Muldoon, and the two hedgehogs scampered off into the night.

"Off you go Ponsonby." said Mrs. Muldoon to her brightly coloured parrot and the parrot flew off into the garden.

Mrs. Muldoon turned to her last pet, Louis. "Right, off you go Louis and don't get lost." she told her pet lion. Louis bounded off into the garden.

Louis was a very old lion and quite harmless. He wouldn't bite anybody. He couldn't even if he wanted to as he had no teeth! Samantha the snake was also very tame and not poisonous, but of course Ted, Paul, and Peter didn't know this!

Back in the different parts of the garden, the three boys were discovering they were on their own. Ted was the first to discover this rather alarming fact when he turned around to speak to his brother only to find Paul was not there. Neither was Peter. A shiver ran down his spine. "Paul.... Pete..." he called in a whisper. There was no reply.
"Paul...Pete..." he called again. Again, there was no reply, but something was moving in the bushes

to his right.

"Cut it out." he whispered. "You can't scare me, Paul."

Again, there was no reply. Ted was getting annoyed now. This was not the place or time to be playing tricks. He was about to pounce on the bushes when, much to his surprise, a donkey's head appeared through the leaves and perched on the donkey's head was a brightly coloured parrot. When he had got over the shock of seeing these two creatures, Ted suddenly felt himself begin to shake. He had remembered what Paul had said he would like to be turned into if Mrs. Muldoon caught him. A horse! Well, a donkey was a kind of horse and Ted was afraid that this donkey in front of him was not a donkey but his brother Paul.

"What has she done to you?" wailed Ted, running up to the donkey and putting his arms round its neck.
Well, Dilys liked this! She didn't meet many people and here was a nice boy hugging her. She licked him on the nose to show him that she liked him.

"Cut it out, Paul" complained Ted, trying to get the donkey to stop licking him. "I've already had one wash today."

Dilys continued to lick her new friend.

"How on earth am I going to explain this to Mam and Dad? I can't take you home and say you're my brother. They'll think I've gone potty!"

Ted remembered Peter and what he wanted to be, if turned into an animal. He looked at the parrot perched on the top of the donkey's head.

"And how am I going to explain to your mother that you're a parrot?" said Ted.
The parrot looked at Ted.

"Speak to me, Peter." begged Ted.
"Who's a pretty boy?" squawked the parrot.
"Say you recognise me old friend," said Ted.
"Ponsonby wants a cracker." squawked the parrot.
"It's me they'll be calling crackers." wailed Ted.
"When I try and tell them that you're a boy and not a parrot!"
Ted sat down to try and think what to do next. He wasn't sitting down long.

"Aarrrrgggghhhh!" he yelled, jumping up quickly holding his bottom.

Two rather squashed looking hedgehogs scampered off into the bushes. Luckily for them, Ted had not put all of his full weight on them when he sat down, or he might have killed the unfortunate creatures.

In another part of the garden his yell of pain was heard by Paul and Peter who had managed to find each other and were now looking for Ted.

"That was Ted's voice." gasped Paul.
"What do you think has happened?" asked a worried Peter.
"I don't know." replied Paul.

Just then, another of Mrs. Muldoon's pets appeared on the path in front of them. They found themselves face to face with Louis the lion.

"Th...th...th...there's a lion in front of us!" stammered Peter.
"Wha.... wha.... what are we going to do?" asked Paul.
"I.... I.... I.... I.... I don't know." stammered back Peter,

wishing they had never come.

Paul suddenly remembered what Ted had said he would want to be if changed into an animal by Mrs. Muldoon. A Lion! Paul at once thought that the lion in front of them was his brother.

"Pete?" he began. "Do you remember what Ted said he wanted to be if Mrs. Muldoon turned him into an animal?"
"Yes." replied Peter, "He said he wanted to be a li……."

Peter didn't finish the sentence.
"You don't mean that lion is…..?" he began.
"It could be." said Paul.
"How do we find out if it's Ted?" asked Peter.
"I don't know." replied his friend. "That's the problem."
Before they could think of a way of proving the lion was or was not Ted, a whistle sounded from somewhere in the garden. On hearing the whistle, the lion turned and disappeared into the night.

"Come back Ted!" yelled Paul. "Quick, Pete, we mustn't lose him."

Both boys charged off down the path after the lion they thought was Ted.

At the same time the lion heard the whistle and ran off, the same thing was happening in another part of the garden. The donkey and parrot on hearing the whistle began to move.
Dilys gave Ted one final lick on the nose and trotted off and the parrot flew off into the night sky.

"Come back, Peter. Come back, Paul." yelled Ted and started to chase after the disappearing donkey.

Try to imagine, if you can, Paul and Peter chasing the lion they thought was Ted, and Ted chasing the Donkey and a parrot he thought was his brother and friend Peter. By the time Ted had arrived at the front door of the house the animals were safely inside. Before Ted could get his breath back, Paul and Peter ran up to join him.

"Ted!" gasped Paul, "You've changed!"
"No, I haven't." replied his brother. "I'm still wearing the same clothes I came out in."
"I don't mean changed your clothes." said Paul.
"What are you on about then?" asked a puzzled

Ted.

"You're no longer a lion." explained Peter.

"A lion?" said Ted. "Have you been drinking?"

"Mrs. Muldoon turned you into a lion….didn't she?" asked Paul.

"She most certainly did not." replied an indignant Ted.

"But we saw you…." began Peter.

"You were stood in front of us." insisted Paul.

"I was not!" replied Ted.

"Do you know what this means?" gulped Peter.

"Yes." said Paul.   "We've been standing and talking to a real lion!"

"Not only that." added Peter. "We've been chasing it through the garden."

"What are you two rambling on about?" asked Ted. "No, don't tell me or I'll end up as daft as you."

Peter and Paul looked at each other unhappily. The thought that they had been chasing a real lion through the garden did not give them a very nice feeling.

"What was it like being a donkey and a parrot?" Ted asked them.

Now it was the other two's turn to look strangely

at Ted. He noticed their stares.

"Now don't try and kid me." he said to them. "I know you were changed into a donkey Paul, and Peter was turned into a parrot."

"I most certainly was not turned into a donkey." replied Paul.

"But you licked me on the nose." Ted told him.

"I have never licked you on the nose." shouted Paul. "Do you think I'm crackers?"

"No." said Ted, "It's Peter who's crackers!"

"Who are you calling crackers?" demanded Peter angrily.

"No, not now," explained Ted. "When you were a parrot, you said Ponsonby wants a cracker."

"I have never said Ponsonby wants a cracker in my life!" snapped Peter angrily.

By now all three boys were having a full-scale argument in front of the house. They were arguing so much that none of them heard the front door open or see a figure come out and stand on the top step. They were still arguing when a voice boomed out stopping them in mid flow.

"Put your hands up or I'll shoot!" it demanded.

The boys turned to face the speaker and found

themselves staring down the barrel of a rusty old shot gun. The gun was being held by Mrs. Muldoon.

"Put up your hands or I'll shoot!" she repeated.

The boys looked at each other and then back at the figure pointing the gun at them. They decided they had better put up their hands as ordered.

"I don't think it's loaded." whispered Ted to the other two.
"I heard that sonny!" snapped Mrs. Muldoon. "I'll show you if it's loaded or not."
She lifted the gun to her shoulder and aimed it at a branch on a nearby tree.

"Do you see that leaf at the end of that branch on that tree?" she asked the boys.
The boys looked at the leaf on the branch on the tree then back to Mrs. Muldoon and nodded.

"You just watch me shoot that leaf off that branch of that tree." she announced.
"She's been watching too many western films on T.V." whispered Paul.
"She must think she's John Wayne." chuckled

Ted.

The boys turned back to look at the leaf on the branch on the tree whilst Mrs. Muldoon prepared to fire. From behind them came a huge explosion which caused them to dive to the ground for safety. A huge cloud of smoke drifted over the garden. The boys struggled to their feet and as the smoke began to clear they looked for the leaf on the branch of the tree that Mrs. Muldoon had been aiming for.

There was no sign of the leaf. There was no sign of the branch, and the tree itself looked as if it might fall over at any time. The boys turned around to face Mrs. Muldoon only to find her flat on her back with her legs waving in the air. The force of the blast from the gun had knocked her off her feet.

At this point the boys could easily have made their escape. Mrs. Muldoon would have been unable to stop them as she was still flat on her back. Instead of making a run for it, all three boys rushed over to help the old lady to her feet.

"Are you alright?" asked Ted as they got her upright.
"I think so, sonny." puffed the old lady.

"Are you sure?" asked Peter.

"I think I must have put too much powder in the gun." chuckled Mrs. Muldoon.

"You must have had enough powder in there to fire a cannon, never mind a shotgun." said Peter.

"It did make quite a big bang, didn't it?" chuckled the old lady.

The three boys helped Mrs. Muldoon into the house and before they realised it, they were inside Sleepy Hollow. They had passed the test for joining the Grizzly Gang, though they had not yet realised that either.

CHAPTER 4

THE BOYS MEET THE ANIMALS

Once inside the house, Mrs. Muldoon led them into her front room and took a seat in an armchair facing the three boys.

"And now perhaps you will tell me what you were doing creeping about my garden in the middle of the night." she said sternly.
"We didn't mean to...." began Paul.
"We weren't going to do any damage." added Peter.
"It was kind of a test of courage." said Ted.
"What do you mean, 'test of courage'?" Mrs. Muldoon asked them.
"Well, it's like this..." began Ted and proceeded to tell her of the test they had to pass before they could become members of the Grizzly Gang.

When Mrs. Muldoon heard the rumour that she was able to turn children into animals she burst into hysterical laughter. She laughed so much that tears ran down her cheeks and she had to hold her sides as they ached from laughing so much. The three boys just looked at her, wondering if she was having a fit.

"I only wish I could turn people into animals." she wheezed. "I'd turn all those idiots down in the Council Offices into sheep and goats."

"Why would you want to do that?" asked Ted.

"You're not from the council, are you?" demanded Mrs. Muldoon.

"No." said Paul. "We're nothing to do with the council."

"Are you telling the truth?" asked the old lady suspiciously. "You've not been sent by them to spy on me?"

"Honest, Mrs. Muldoon." promised Peter. "We're nothing to do with the council. we're still in school."

"Then you'd better tell me who you are." she told them.

"I'm Ted Thomas." said Ted. "And this is my brother Paul and our friend Peter."

"I see." said Mrs. Muldoon, sounding more friendly now. "I'm glad you're not from the council."

"Why don't you like the council?" asked Peter.

"Crikey." said Paul before Mrs. Muldoon could answer Peter's question. "Look at the time."

"It's nine o'clock" groaned Ted. "Dad will do his nut. We're going to be late."

"Can I make a suggestion?" said Mrs. Muldoon.

"Anything you can suggest to keep us out of

trouble with our Dad would be appreciated." said Ted.

"Why don't you stay here for the night?" began Mrs. Muldoon. "I'd have to telephone your parents to see if it would be alright though."

"It's a good idea," said Paul.

"Yes." said Ted. "If we don't go home, he won't be able to give us a row."

"Right." said Mrs. Muldoon. "If you write your telephone number on this piece of paper and Peter writes his on this piece, I'll go and ring them."

The boys wrote their numbers on the pieces of paper and gave them back to Mrs. Muldoon who took them and went out to the telephone. The boys waited impatiently for her to return. It seemed like ages before she came back into the room.

"What did they say?" asked Paul as she came back into the room.

"Both your parents said you could stay." she announced.

"Great." said Ted.

"Ted, your father asked me to give you a message." she told him.

"What did he say?" asked Ted.

"He said to be sure to behave yourself." smiled
Mrs. Muldoon.

"Bloomin' cheek." muttered Ted.

"It's very good of you to let us stay the night." said
Paul.

"That's quite all right." said Mrs. Muldoon. "You'll
be company for Louis and his friends.

"Louis and his friends?" said Ted. "I didn't know
any other people lived with you."

"Oh, Louis and his friends are not people."
laughed Mrs. Muldoon.

"Not people?" gulped Peter. "What are they
then?"

"They're my pets," explained Mrs. Muldoon.
"Would you like to meet them?"

"Of course we would." said Paul politely.

Ted looked at Paul.

"You don't think she's potty, do you?" he
whispered.

"Sshhh!" whispered back Paul. "Don't be rude."

"I'll call them." said Mrs. Muldoon. "Oh Louis,
come to Mummy."

The boys were wondering what kind of animal
Louis could be when into the room padded a
Lion. You never saw three boys move so quickly

in your lives. Ted dived under the table, Paul climbed onto the cupboard while Peter climbed into the cupboard and slammed the door behind him.

"This is...." began Mrs. Muldoon, turning round to the boys to find they had disappeared.
"That's funny." she said to herself. "They were here a minute ago, I wonder where they could have gone?"
She looked round the room but could see no sign of the boys.

"Oh, boys, where are you?" come out and meet Louis."
"But he's a lion." said Ted from under the table.
"Of course he's a lion." said Mrs. Muldoon. "And what are you doing under the table?"
"Isn't he dangerous?" asked Paul from on top of the cupboard.
"Of course not." laughed Mrs. Muldoon. "And what are you doing on top of my cupboard?
"Doesn't he bite?" asked Peter, peering out from inside the cupboard. "No." said Mrs. Muldoon. "He couldn't even if he wanted to. He's got no teeth!
"Come out, you're all quite safe."

Slowly, the boys came out from their hiding

places and nervously made friends with Louis.

"But how does he eat his food if he's got no teeth?" asked Paul, nervously stroking the lion.
"Oh, he's got a pair of false teeth he wears at mealtimes." explained Mrs. Muldoon.
"Pardon?" said Ted.
"He has a pair of false teeth he wears at mealtimes." repeated Mrs. Muldoon.
"False teeth!" exclaimed Ted.
"Of course." said Mrs. Muldoon. "What's strange about that?"
"I think she is potty." whispered Ted to the other two.
"Ah, here's Henry and Henrietta." announced Mrs. Muldoon, and into the room scampered two rather squashed looking hedgehogs.
"Henry and Henrietta hedgehog!" spluttered Peter, trying not to laugh.
"What has happened to you?" asked Mrs. Muldoon picking up the little creatures. "You look a bit squashed. I wish you could talk and tell me what happened to you."

Ted was rather glad they could not talk as he has been the one to squash them!

"Ah, here comes Ponsonby." announced Mrs.

Muldoon as a parrot flew into the room.
"Ponsonby? He's called Ponsonby?" asked Ted
trying to keep a straight face.
"What's wrong with the name Ponsonby?" asked
Mrs. Muldoon.
"Nothing." said Ted quickly, not wanting to offend
the old lady.
"Who's a pretty boy?" squawked the parrot.
"You wouldn't happen to have pet donkey,
would you?" asked Ted remembering the one
that he'd met in the garden.
"Why yes." said Mrs. Muldoon. "That's Dilys."

At that moment, into the room trotted Dilys. She
recognised Ted as the nice boy she'd made
friends with in the garden and trotted over to him
and started licking him on the nose.

"Gerr off, Dilys." objected Ted.
"Oh, she likes you." said Mrs. Muldoon. "I'm so
glad."
"Looks like Dilys fancies you." laughed Paul as
the donkey continued to lick Ted.
"Shup up." snapped Ted. "You're only jealous."
"Oh, there's no need to be jealous, Paul." pointed
out Mrs. Muldoon. "Samantha seems to have
become quite attached to you."
"Samantha? attached? where? how…?"

stammered Paul.

"Why there." said Mrs. Muldoon, pointing to Paul's leg, around which was coiled Samantha.

"S...S...S...Snake!" spluttered Paul.

"That's Samantha" explained Mrs. Muldoon. "Don't worry, she's quite harmless."

"She's legless as well as armless" chuckled Ted.

"Oh, keep quiet!" snapped Paul not at all amused by his brothers' joke.

"If you look after my pets, I'll go and get you some supper." Mrs. Muldoon said leaving the room.

The boys were left with the animals.

Dilys still licking Ted on the nose, Samantha still coiled round Paul's leg and Ponsonby perched on Peter's head.

"What do you think?" asked Paul.

"I think she's rather odd to say the least," said Ted. "And stop licking me, Dilys." he added.

"I wonder why she doesn't like the council?" asked Peter.

"I'll ask her when she comes back." said Ted.

A short while later, Mrs. Muldoon returned carrying a tray of sandwiches and glasses of squash for the boys, which they proceeded to

devour with Ted trying to stop Dilys eating his
sandwiches!

"Why don't you like the council?" asked Ted.
"I'll tell you about that in the morning." promised
Mrs. Muldoon. "It's getting rather late. I think you
should get off to bed. If you follow me, I'll take
you to your bedroom."

The boys followed Mrs. Muldoon out of the front
room, across the hall and up the grand flight of
stairs. They walked behind her across the
landing to a door which she opened, and they
followed her inside. Inside the bedroom was the
biggest bed the boys had ever seen. It was an
old fashioned four-poster bed with a large
canopy above it.

Mrs. Muldoon crossed to a large wardrobe,
opened it, took something out of it and brought it
to the boys.

"You'd better have these to wear in bed." she told
them.

She handed them three old fashioned nightshirts,
the type you slip on over your head. The boys
thanked her, and she left them to settle down for

the night. They undressed and put on the nightshirts. Paul looked at his brother and Peter dressed in this strange nightwear and burst out laughing.

"What are you laughing at?" asked Ted.

"You and Peter." chuckled Paul. "You should see what you look like in those nightshirts."

The two boys went over to a mirror to look at themselves and had to admit they did look funny.

"You don't look any better." pointed out Peter, and Paul had to agree with him.

"Bagsie in the middle." yelled Ted, jumping into the four-poster bed.

Peter got in one side of him and Paul the other. Although it was quite a big bed it was not all that big when there were three boys trying to settle down. Ted was quite happy in the middle but both Peter and Paul either side of him were rather close to the edge of the bed.

"I'm very close to the edge." pointed out Paul.

"What was that? "asked Ted turning to face his brother.

"I'm...." and before he could say anymore, Paul

disappeared off the edge of the bed with a yell.

Ted and Peter thought this was hilarious. Paul, however, did not.

"You did that on purpose." he yelled at Ted as he got up off the floor.

"Sorry." apologised Ted who wasn't really.

"You've asked for this." threatened Paul and, running round to the other side of the bed, he got in next to Peter and gave him an almighty shove.

Peter rolled onto Ted who rolled off the bed and onto the floor just as Paul had done. This time it was Paul who joined Peter in the hysterical laughter as Ted clambered off the floor.

"This is war!" declared Ted, charging round the bed and diving in next to Paul.

"Wait .... aaghhhh!" yelled Peter as he was pushed out of the bed to go tumbling onto the floor like the other two before him.

"You've asked for this." he shouted picking himself up and grabbing a pillow.

"Pillow Fight!" yelled Ted picking up another pillow while his brother picked up a third pillow.

"Death to the pusher outer!" yelled Peter swinging his pillow round his head and aiming at

Ted.

Ted tried to dodge the blow, but he was standing on the bed and did not have a firm grip. Peter's pillow caught him smack in face and he tumbled onto the bed and off it onto the floor with a yell.

"Good shot, Pete." Paul congratulated him.

But Peter did not hear him as he was already swinging the pillow to attack Paul.

"Hold on." began Paul. "I'm on your ...."
Whoomph!
The pillow smashed into his face, and he too went tumbling backwards off the bed and onto the floor as Ted was trying to get up. They both went tumbling back on the floor.
"Yeah!" yelled Peter triumphantly.

His triumph did not last long as Ted and Paul decided to team up and take their revenge on their friend. They advanced towards Peter who backed away nervously.

"Now boys." he began. "Two against one is not fair!"

Ted and Paul ignored him and continued to advance on him.

"Take no prisoners." yelled Ted.

Both he and Paul charged at the unfortunate Peter and began attacking him with their pillows. "Mercy!" begged Peter, trying without success to defend himself.
"No mercy!" yelled Ted, continuing with the attack.

Peter stood no chance, and he was soon flat on the floor as the blows continued to rain down on him. The two brothers were enjoying themselves and neither noticed that Ted's pillow had a small tear in it which was getting bigger and bigger with every blow he struck. Before they knew it the pillow burst open, and thousands and thousands of feathers went sailing into the air. The bedroom looked as if it was in the middle of a blizzard as the feathers floated about the room. The mishap brought the pillow fight to an end as all three boys looked in amazement at the scene.

"Oh dear." said Ted, "That's torn it."
"You're the one that's torn it." pointed out his brother, pointing to the now empty pillowcase

that Ted was holding.

"I didn't mean for it to happen." said Ted.

"What are you going to do?" asked Peter.

"We'll have to pick them all up." said Paul.

"It'll take us all night." complained Ted.

"Well, we can't leave it like this." said Paul. "And you can be the one to tell Mrs. Muldoon about what happened in the morning."

"Why me?" groaned Ted.

"It was your pillow that burst." pointed our Peter.

"You'll have to help me." said Ted.

Of course, the other two boys did help him, but it took a very long time and when they had at last picked up all of the feathers they could find, they climbed wearily into bed. They were so tired that there was no more fun and games that night and soon the three of them were fast asleep.

CHAPTER 5

COUNCIL of WAR

The following morning, Ted was the first to wake up. He was woken up by a very strange sensation on his feet. He sat up in bed and for a moment had forgotten where he was. The sight of a donkey licking his feet gave him quite a turn. Then he realised where he was and the donkey licking his feet was Dilys.

"Oh, it's you Dilys." he yawned. "Is it time to get up?"

He got out of bed and got dressed. Peter and Paul awoke and started to dress also.

"I wonder where Mrs. Muldoon is." said Ted.
"Cooking breakfast by the smell of it." replied Paul sniffing at the smell of bacon cooking that was wafting upstairs.
"Let's go then." said Ted. "I could eat a horse! Sorry Dilys." He apologised to the donkey when he realised what he had said.
"Lead the way Dilys." said Peter.

Dilys seemed to understand the instruction and

led them out of the bedroom, across the landing, and down the stairs. She trotted into the kitchen with the three boys behind her.
Mrs. Muldoon was cooking breakfast.

"Good morning, boys." she welcomed them. "Sit down. Breakfast is nearly ready."

The boys took their seat at the table and Mrs. Muldoon served them plates of bacon and egg. It smelt delicious.

"Tuck in." she instructed them.

The boys didn't need telling twice and soon there were three empty plates on the table and three full stomachs in the boys.

"I think we ought to apologise for creeping round your garden last night." began Paul.
"There's no need to," said Mrs. Muldoon. "There's no harm done, and everything has turned out alright. I don't get many visitors, and your visit has meant a lot to me."
"Perhaps we could come and visit you every week." suggested Ted.
"I'd really like that." replied Mrs. Muldoon. "But I'm afraid that won't be possible."

"Why not?" asked Ted.

"Because of the council." replied the old lady.

"How can the council stop us coming to visit you?" asked Peter puzzled by her answer.

"Let me explain from the beginning." said Mrs. Muldoon. "You probably know that the council are planning to build a by-pass round the village because all the heavy traffic is damaging houses in the village."

"Yes." said Peter, "I've heard my parents talking about it."

Ted and Paul nodded in agreement.

"But how does that stop us coming to visit you?" asked Paul.

"They plan to build the new road through the wood and my house is in the way." said Mrs. Muldoon. "They're going to knock down my house."

"But they can't do that without your permission, surely?" asked Ted.

"I'm afraid they can." answered Mrs. Muldoon. "They have a compulsory purchase order for my house which means I have to sell it to them."

"Where will you live?" asked Peter.

"They offered me a bungalow on the new housing estate the other side of the village." Mrs.

Muldoon told him.

"Perhaps we could come and visit you there." suggested Ted.

"You could if I were going to live there, but I'm not." said Mrs. Muldoon defiantly.

"Why not?" asked Paul.

"They won't let me take my pets with me," she explained, "and if they can't come with me, I'm not leaving."

"But you can't stay here when they knock the house down. You might get killed." said Ted, worried that Mrs. Muldoon would be hurt.

"I'm going to lock myself in, load up my gun and wait for them to arrive." she told the boys.

The boys looked at each other. There was no way Mrs. Muldoon would be allowed to stop the by-pass. Ted had visions of her taking pot-shots at the council workers, being arrested by the police, and being sent to prison. They couldn't let that happen to her.

"Perhaps we could go to the Council and explain the situation." said Ted.

"Yes, we'll go first thing Monday morning." added Paul.

"You can if you like." said Mrs. Muldoon. "But I think you will be wasting your time. Once the council have decided to do something, they won't change their minds."

"They haven't met us yet." said Ted.

"We'd better be going now Mrs. Muldoon." said Paul.

"We'll come and tell you how we got on at the Council Offices after we've been there." said Ted.

The boys said goodbye to Mrs. Muldoon and the animals and Dilys gave Ted a goodbye kiss. As they walked through the woods towards the village, they discussed the problem and how they would go about trying to solve it. As they came to the Swing Tree, they saw a number of the Grizzly Gang sitting under it. The gang were surprised to see them.

"You're up early this morning." said John as they walked over to join them. "How did you get on last night?" he asked winking at the others.

"Fine." said Paul. "Everything went just fine."

"You don't mean you actually went to Sleepy Hollow?" asked Gary in amazement.

"Of course we did." said Peter. "That's what you said we had to do."

"In fact, we did more than just go there." announced Ted.

"What did you do?" asked Vincent.

"We stayed there all night." Ted said proudly.

"You never did," said Gwyn.

"We did." said Paul.

"I don't believe you." said John. "No one in their right mind would stay in the garden of Sleepy Hollow all night."

"We didn't stay there." said Paul.

"But you just said you did!" shouted John angrily.

"I said we stayed there all night. I didn't say we stayed in the garden all night." explained Ted.

"I suppose you stayed in the house." John said sarcastically.

"That's exactly what we did do." replied Ted, smiling.

The gang stood open-mouthed at this bit of news.

"I don't believe you." said John.

"You can easily check." Paul informed him. "Ask my mother or Peter's. They'll confirm it."

"We're just on the way home now." said Ted. "Come and check if you want to."

"When do we become members?" asked Peter.

"We'll let you know." said John sullenly.

"O.K," said Paul. "and if you want proof, you can always go and ask Mrs. Muldoon, she'll tell you we were there."

With this, the three boys left the gang at the Swing Tree and made their way home. On reaching the village they split up agreeing to meet on Monday and go to the Council Offices to try and help Mrs. Muldoon.

When Ted and Paul got home, they found their parents anxious to learn what they had been doing. No one in the village really knew Mrs. Muldoon and both Mr. and Mrs. Thomas were keen to find out a bit more about the old lady.

Ted and Paul told them about staying in the old four-poster bed and wearing nightshirts. They left out the pillow fight and the burst pillow. They told their parents about the animals but did not mention one of them was a lion and another a snake. They were afraid their parents would not let them go there if they thought there were dangerous animals at Sleepy Hollow. They told them about the plan to demolish the house and how Mrs. Muldoon did not want to leave, and Ted asked his father if there was any way Mrs. Muldoon could stay in her old house.

"Not really, son." said his father. "If the council have a compulsory purchase order on her house, she has to sell it to them."

"Then there's nothing we can do?" asked Paul.

"There might be something." replied his father. "As you know the new road is planned to go through the wood and Sleepy Hollow and pass very close to your school. I don't think that is the best route."

"Where else could they build it?" asked Ted, showing interest.

"Well," continued his father. "If they were to take it along the old railway line, there would be no need to take it through the wood or knock down Sleepy Hollow."

"Why haven't they planned it that way?" asked Paul.

"I don't know." said Mr. Thomas. "I think it would be much cheaper to build that way and they would not have to knock down all those trees."

"How can we get them to change the route?" asked Ted.

"Easier said than done." admitted Mr. Thomas. "Once they start work, they will not change their minds."

"But they haven't started yet." pointed out Paul.

"But they're due to start very soon." said his father.

"Can't you do anything?" asked Ted.

"Well, I can't stop the work, but I will have a word with the Clerk of the council on Monday."

promised Mr. Thomas.

"That would be great, Dad," said Ted.

"Don't build up your hopes too much." warned his father.

"It might be too late to stop them."

"Not if we can help it." thought Ted. "Not if we can help it."

CHAPTER 6

A DEMONSTRATION

"I've had a great idea." announced Ted.

"Oh no!" groaned his brother. "Not another one of your ideas."

"And what's wrong with my ideas?" asked Ted.

"They always go wrong and get us into trouble." said Paul.

"This one won't." promised Ted.

"Famous last words." said Paul, not at all convinced. "Well, come on then, what is this great idea of yours?"

"You'll have to wait until we get to Peter's." Ted announced.

The two boys left to call for Peter. When they arrived, he took them down to the shed at the bottom of the garden where they would not be disturbed. They told him about what their father had said and how he was going to contact the Clerk and see if the route of the by-pass could be changed.

"That would be great." said Peter. "But isn't there anything we can do to help Mrs. Muldoon?"

"There is." announced Ted. "I've had a great idea."

"Here we go." thought Paul, dreading what crazy idea his brother was going to come up with this time.

"And just what is this great idea?" he asked his brother.

"When people object to something they have a demonstration." said Ted.

"I hope you don't mean what I think you mean." groaned Paul.

"I think we should have a demonstration outside the Council Offices." said Ted.

"I was afraid you were going to say that." said his brother.

"And what's wrong with having a demonstration?" asked Ted, annoyed with his brother for not being more enthusiastic.

"When people demonstrate there are usually hundreds of them." pointed out Peter.

"So what." said Ted.

"There's only three of us." said Paul. "You can't have a demonstration with only three people."

"I don't see why not" argued Ted. "Surely anything that might help Mrs. Muldoon should be tried?"

"He's got a point." admitted Peter.

"A demonstration would certainly bring the matter to the public's attention."

"You could be right." agreed Paul reluctantly.

"Perhaps we should give it a try. O.K. Ted, what's the plan?"

"Wherever you see a demonstration on T.V." said Ted, "they always have signs with slogans written on them."

"That's a good idea." said Paul, becoming more enthusiastic with the idea. "But where would we get the wood to make the signs and paint to write the slogans?"

"That's no problem." said Peter, pointing to a pile of wood and cans of paint in the corner of the shed.

"Won't your father mind?" asked Paul.

"No, said Peter. "That stuff has been there for months. "If he were going to use it, he would have by now."

"Let's get started then," said Ted.

They began work, finding a selection of tools in the shed which they used to make their signs. Peter would not have been so keen to volunteer the wood and paint for the job if he had known what it was in the shed for. His father had bought the wood to make some new kitchen cabinets for his wife and the paint was for decorating the front room of the house. Unfortunately, Peter did not know this, and the three boys set to work. For the next half-hour there came from the shed the sound of wood being sawed and nails being hammered and the sound of an occasional yell as Ted's hammer landed on his fingernail instead of a metal nail! Thirty minutes and few sore fingernails later, the signs were complete, except for their slogans.

"What are we going to write on them?" asked Peter.
"I think we should each make up our own slogans." suggested Ted.
"Good idea." agreed Paul. "Let's get on with it."

The tins of paint were opened, and Peter found a new packet of brushes and gave them out. They each found it hard to think of the slogans but eventually they had all written something on their signs.

"What have you written?" Ted asked his brother.

Paul turned his sign to the other two for them to read his slogan. Written in large red letters was:

**DON'T CHOP
DOWN
OUR WOOD**

"That's a good slogan." Ted congratulated his brother. "What have you written Pete?"

Peter turned his sign round to display his slogan:

DON'T DEMOLISH
SLEEPY HOLLOW

"Nice one, Peter," said Ted.
"And what have you written?" asked Paul.

Proudly, Ted turned his sign round. Paul and Peter looked at the sign and then at each other.

"Well, what do you think?" asked Ted.

Written on his sign in large red letters was:

DON'T LET
THE COUNCIL
DESTROY DILYS!

"Well, what do you think?" he asked again.
"It should get people talking." said Paul.
"Yes." agreed Peter. "They'll wonder who on earth Dilys is for a start."
"That's part of the plan." chuckled Ted.

"Can we leave the signs here until tomorrow morning?" asked Paul.

"Of course." said Peter. "We can collect them when we go to the Council Offices for our demonstration."

Monday morning arrived and Ted and Paul were up and dressed and downstairs by half-past seven, much to the amazement of their parents.

"What is the matter with you two?" asked their mother.

"What do you mean?" asked Ted.

"You are never up this early in the morning." she pointed out.

"We've got a lot to do today," said Paul.

"We'll just have cereal for breakfast this morning." said Ted, "No time for a cooked breakfast."

"What?!" exclaimed Mr. Thomas, looking up from his newspaper.

"No cooked breakfast? I can't remember that ever happening before."

"I don't know what's got into these two lately." said Mrs. Thomas.

The boys started shovelling spoonfuls of cereal into their mouths, only to be told by their mother to eat their breakfast properly. They slowed down a little, but not much and were soon finished and up from the table and heading for the door.

"Make sure you stay out of tr......"

Mr. Thomas' words were lost as the door slammed behind the two boys.

The boys quickly made their way to Peter's house where they collected their three signs from the garden shed and then all three of them made their way to the Council Offices which was in the main street of the village. They were early and the offices had not yet opened so they had to wait for the workers to arrive. When the workers began to arrive, Ted, Paul, and Peter began their demonstration walking up and down waving their signs. The people going into the offices looked at the slogans written on the signs with some amusement. Ted's sign in particular got a lot of attention with a number of people coming over to ask him who Dilys was. On hearing it was a donkey they went away laughing.

Members of the public began to arrive and then Paul spotted someone coming towards them.

"Look out." he warned. "It's the police."
A policeman had just got out of his police car
and was walking towards them.

"Hello, hello, hello." said Ted as the policeman
came up to them.
"Are you trying to be funny lad?" asked the
policeman.
"No sir." Ted replied quickly.
"And just what are you doing here?" he asked the
boys.
"Having a demonstration." said Paul.
"Well, I'm afraid you can't." the policeman
informed them.
"Why not?" asked Peter.
"Because someone has complained you are
making a nuisance of yourselves." replied the
policeman.
"I see." said Ted, turning and walking towards the
Council Offices. "Come on you two." he called to
Paul and Peter.
"Where are we going?" asked Paul.
"If we can't demonstrate outside, we'll
demonstrate inside." called back Ted.

The policeman watched as Ted led the way into
the building followed by the other two boys. He
shook his head, smiled, and went back to his car

and drove off.

The boys, on entering the building, found themselves in an entrance hall with a number of rooms leading off it. Ted looked around and saw one of the doors had the word INFORMATION written on it in capital letters. They walked over to it and Ted knocked the door.

"Come in." called the voice from the other side of the door, and the boys went in.

Sitting behind a desk in the middle of the office sat an important looking lady. The boys went over and stood Infront of the desk.

"What can I do for you?" the lady asked the boys.

"We'd like to see the Clerk please." replied Ted politely.

"Do you have an appointment?" the lady asked him.

"I thought you only had appointments with the doctors or the dentists." said Ted.

"Do you have an appointment?" the lady asked again.

"No, we don't." replied Paul.

"If you don't have an appointment, you can't see the Clerk." explained the lady.

"We're not leaving until we see him." announced

Ted and sat down on the floor. Peter and Paul did the same.

"What are you doing?" asked the lady.

"We're having a sit in." explained Ted, "And we're not leaving until we've seen the Clerk."

"You can't sit down on the floor like that." said the lady sounding a little worried.

"We want the Clerk... We want the Clerk..." chanted Ted, with Peter and Paul joining in.

"Please be quiet." said the lady, getting flustered.

"We want the Clerk... we want the Clerk..." shouted the three boys even louder.

By now the lady began to panic. She picked up the phone, dialled a number and waited for the ringing phone to be picked up in another office.

"Mr. James?" she spoke into the mouthpiece. "This is Mrs. Osbourne in Information. Could you come down here? I have a problem".

She put the phone down and the boys continued to chant.

"We want the Clerk...we want the Clerk..."

Suddenly the door was pushed open, and a man rushed into the room. He didn't get very far because he tripped over Ted's sign and went crashing to the floor.

"What's going on here?" he demanded, picking himself up from the floor.

"Did you enjoy your trip?" Ted asked him.

The man glared at Ted and then looked at Mrs. Osbourne for an explanation.

"It's these boys." began Mrs. Osbourne. "They refuse to leave until they've seen the Clerk."
"Oh, do they?" said Mr. James turning to face the three boys still sitting on the floor. "Now look here…"
"We want the Clerk… We want the Clerk…," shouted the boys.
"Quiet!" yelled Mr. James.
"WE WANT THE CLERK…WE WANT THE CLERK…" yelled the boys, even louder.
"QUIET!" yelled Mr. James.
The boys went quiet.

"Now perhaps you will tell me what this nonsense is all about." demanded Mr. James.
"Are you the Clerk?" asked Ted.
"No." replied Mr. James, I'm……
"WE WANT THE CLERK…WE WANT THE CLERK…" yelled the boys.

"He's not here." shouted Mr. James.
The boys went quiet again.

"Where is he then?" asked Ted.
"That's none of your business." snapped Mr.
James. "Now tell me what this is all about."

The boys between them explained why they
were there and that they were trying to save Mrs.
Muldoon's house from being demolished. Mr.
James was not helpful at all. He told them they
could not go around demanding changes to the
plans that had already been made just because
some stubborn old lady did not want to leave her
home.

"Besides." continued Mr. James. "Only the Clerk
could stop the work starting and he won't be
back until Wednesday."
"We'll see him then then." said Ted.
"You'll be too late." laughed Mr. James. "Work is
due to start this morning, and once it starts,
nothing will be able to stop it, not even the Clerk.
That old woman's house will be just a pile of
rubble by this time tomorrow."
"Not if we can help it." said Ted defiantly. "Come
on boys." he said to the other two. "There's
nothing more we can do here. Mrs. Muldoon will

need all our help back at the house."
Picking up their signs they left the Council
Offices and made their way slowly up the main
street.

"What are we going to do?" asked Paul. "There's
no way we can stop the work starting."
"I wouldn't be too sure of that." said Ted.
"What do you mean?" asked Peter.
"I've got another great idea." announced Ted.
"Oh, no!" groaned Paul. "Not another one."
"What is it?" asked Peter.
"I'll tell you as we go to the work-camp." said
Ted.
"Why are we going there?" asked Paul.
"You'll see." said Ted mysteriously.

They walked on down the main street, dumping
their signs in a litterbin. At the end of the main
street, they crossed the road and made their way
to the work-camp that had been set up just
outside the village. The work-camp was a large
fenced off area where the council workmen kept
all the equipment they would need when they
began work on the by-pass.
As well as large equipment such as bulldozers
and J.C.Bs, there were large amounts of tools
and building materials that would be needed to

complete the new road. As they were approaching it Ted had explained his plan to the other two.

"You know." said Paul with a smile, "It's so crazy, it might just work."
"You could be right" agreed Peter.
"Of course it will work." Ted said confidently.

They walked on until they reached the perimeter fence which ran round the work-camp. They could see there were only two workmen on the site. This would make Ted's plan easier to carry out. The boys went over to the two workmen who were on a tea-break.

"Hello, what do you want?" asked one of the workmen as the boys walked over.
"Nothing." replied Ted. "Just came over to see how you are getting on with the work."
"Are you the only two working here?" asked Peter.
"At the moment." the man replied. "We're waiting for the driver of the bulldozer to arrive so we can start knocking down some trees."
"Rather you than me." said Paul.
"Why's that?" asked the man. "We're not afraid of hard work."

"Oh, it's not the hard work we'd be frightened of," said Ted. "It's the......no, you wouldn't be interested."

"Go on." said the man. "Just a minute, I want my mate to hear this. Bert, come here a minute will you," he called to his colleague.

"What is it, Harry?" asked the man crossing to join them.

"These kids were going to tell me something and I thought you should hear it as well." said Harry.

"Go on lad. Tell us."

"Well, you probably won't believe me." said Ted.

"Go on, tell us." insisted Bert.

"Well"....began Ted, "....No, you won't believe me."

"Tell us." said Harry.

"Haven't you heard of the headless phantoms?" asked Ted.

"Headless what?" asked Bert.

"Headless phantoms." repeated Ted.

"No." said Harry. "What about them?"

"A hundred years ago," explained Ted, "they lived in Sleepy Hollow, but they died in mysterious circumstances."

"Gosh!" said Bert.

"Some people say they were murdered." added Paul.

"M...m...murdered?" stammered Bert.

"Murdered" repeated Peter.

"But how does this concern us?" asked Bert.

"Well, since their death." continued Ted, "they are supposed to roam the woods by day as well as by night, and it's said that anyone that cuts down even a single tree, or tries to damage Sleepy Hollow, is carried off and never seen again."

"Did you hear that, Bert?" Harry asked his friend.

"Yes Harry." replied Bert. "Do you believe it?"

"I don't know." said Harry.

"There are three headless phantoms altogether." said Ted.

"Oh my goodness!" said Bert.

"They're not the only ghosts that haunt these woods." said Paul.

"You mean there are more?" gulped Harry.

"Oh, yes." said Peter, taking over the story. "There are two animals that also prowl the woods."

"Oh, that's alright," said Bert. "Animals won't do us much harm."

"I wouldn't be too sure of that," said Ted.

"What do you mean?" asked Harry.

"One of the animals is a snake, and the other a lion." Ted told him.

Harry shivered and Bert turned white.

"Well, we must be going." announced Ted. "Look after yourselves."

"Do you have to go already?" asked a rather nervous Bert.

"Wouldn't you like to stay for a cup of tea?" asked Harry.

"No thank you." replied Paul. "We don't like to stay in the woods too long, just in case."

"In case of what?" asked Bert.

"In case the headless phantoms appear of course." explained Peter.

"See you, I hope." said Ted.

The three boys left the work-camp and the two very worried workmen walked back to Sleepy Hollow to report to Mrs. Muldoon. Bert and Harry watched them go and minutes later they were left alone at the work-camp. They looked at each other.

"Do you think there is any truth in the story they told us Bert?" Harry asked his friend.

"I don't think so." replied Bert. "I think they were just trying to scare us."

"I am scared Bert." said Harry.

"Forget about it." said Bert. "Let's have another cup of tea."

The two workmen brewed up for another cup of tea but each of them kept looking nervously into

the trees and bushes that surrounded the work-
camp.

The three boys arrived back at Sleepy Hollow
and told Mrs. Muldoon what had happened at
the Council Offices.

"Then I'm going to lose my house and animals."
sobbed Mrs. Muldoon, beginning to cry.
"Not if we can help it." said Ted.
"Don't cry Mrs. Muldoon." said Paul. "Ted has a
plan and I think it just might work."
"What do you mean, 'just might work'?" asked
Ted. "Of course it's going to work."
"What is this plan?" asked Mrs. Muldoon.
Ted began to tell her the idea he had had to slow
down the work, and so hopefully save her house.
When he'd finished explaining she did seem a
little more cheerful.
"It'll mean we have to stay here for the next two
nights." said Paul.
"That's no problem as long as your parents give
their permission." said Mrs. Muldoon.
"I'll go and ring them now." said Paul.
"And I'll come with you and ring my mother." said
Peter.
"You tell Mrs. Muldoon the rest of the plan." said
Paul.

While Paul and Peter went to make the phone calls, Ted explained everything to Mrs. Muldoon.

"Can we borrow Louis and Samantha for half an hour?" he asked her when he'd finished telling her the whole plan.
"What for?" asked the old lady, a bit concerned.
"We'd like to take them for a walk." said Ted.
"We'll look after them I promise."
"I know you will." said Mrs. Muldoon. "Of course you can take them for a walk."
"They wouldn't hurt anyone would they?" asked Ted.
"No." laughed Mrs. Muldoon. "They're quite harmless."

Paul and Peter returned with the news that permission had been granted for them all to stay with Mrs. Muldoon for the next two nights.
"Dad said to make sure you behave yourself." Paul told his brother.
"He's always saying that!" complained Ted. "Anyone would think I was always misbehaving."
Paul said nothing.

Now they could get down to some serious planning for the battle ahead.

CHAPTER 7

OPERATION PHANTOM

The boys began to get ready for the first part of Ted's plan.
Mrs. Muldoon brought Louis' collar and lead ready for the walk.

"We have a slight problem." pointed out Peter.
"What's that?" asked Ted.
"How do you take a snake for a walk? It hasn't got any legs."
"We'll take her for a slither then." Ted laughed.
"Just carry her." suggested Mrs. Muldoon.
"I wish someone would carry me when I have to go for a walk." smiled Ted.
"Do we need anything else?" asked Peter.
"Yes." said Ted. "Three night-shirts from upstairs."

Peter went to fetch them.

"Are you sure it's alright for us to cut a small hole in each of them?" Ted asked Mrs. Muldoon.
"Of course." replied the old lady. "You've got to be able to see where you are going."

Peter returned with the three nightshirts.

The boys proceeded to tie the neck part of each so the head could not be pushed through it. They each put on their nightshirt and Mrs. Muldoon began cutting a small hole in each so that they boys could look out and see where they were going. This done, the nightshirts were taken off and they prepared to leave for Operation Phantom.

They set off towards the work-camp with Paul carrying the nightshirts, Peter carrying Samantha and Ted leading Louis.

Mrs. Muldoon watched them go until they disappeared into the trees. None of the boys spoke as they walked towards the work-camp. As they neared it, Ted began to go over the details of the plan to make sure there were no mistakes.

"We'll leave the animals here." said Ted as they reached a clearing. "I'll tie Louis' lead to this tree. Samantha won't stray far from him."
"What do we do?" asked Peter.
"We'll circle round and come in from the other side." explained Ted.
"I get the idea" smiled Paul. "We'll scare them, and they will come running right towards the

animals."

"Right." said Ted. "Now quietly does it, follow me."

He led the way through the trees round the outskirts of the work-camp until they were on the opposite side to the animals. They quickly and quietly slipped on their phantom disguises. They were really good having tied the neck, it gave the appearance of there being no heads, just what they wanted. They could see through the holes that had been cut in the nightshirts. While this was going on, Bert and Harry were coming to the end of yet another tea break.

"Bert." began Harry.

"What is it, Harry?" asked Bert.

"I've been thinking about those headless phantoms." said Harry.

"What about them Harry?" asked Bert.

"What if they did come after us?" asked Harry.

"You didn't believe those boys, did you?" asked his companion.

Just at that moment, the boys rustled the bush behind which they were hiding.

"What was that?" asked Harry, jumping up.

"What was what?" asked Bert.

"I heard a rustling sound in those bushes." replied Harry, pointing at the bushes.

"I didn't hear anything." said his friend. "Sit down and drink your tea."

Harry sat down again but kept his eyes on the bushes. The bushes rustled again. Once more Harry shot to his feet.

"There it is again." he whispered.

"I heard it that time." said Bert, also standing.

"Perhaps it was the wind."

"Ooooooh......Oooooooooh......" wailed Ted from behind the bushes.

"Wh....wh...wh...what was that?" stuttered Harry.

"Perhaps it was an owl." suggested Bert.

"It couldn't have been an owl, Bert." pointed out Harry. "They don't come out during the day, they are asleep."

"Perhaps it couldn't get to sleep." suggested his friend.

"It didn't sound like an owl." said Harry.

"Ooooooh......Oooooooooh......Oooooooooh....." the three boys took up the moaning.

"I'm scared Bert." wailed Harry.

"So am I Harry." wailed Bert.

This was the moment the three phantoms

decided to emerge from their hiding place. They pushed through the bushes to stand before the two workmen, groaning and moaning.

"L....l....look, Bert" stammered Harry.
"I am l....l....looking." replied Bert.
"It's the headless phantoms." shrieked Harry.
"Run for your life." wailed Bert.
Bert had already turned and was running away from the three ghosts as fast as he could go. Harry did not exactly hang about. With a yell of terror he was off after his friend as fast as he could go. The boys continued to moan under the nightshirts but now there was a considerable amount of giggling. They took off their disguises.

"Shall we follow them?" asked Pete.
"No." said Ted. "We'd better wait here. They're bound to panic and come dashing back this way when they run into Louis and Samantha."
"I'd love to see their faces when they meet them." chuckled Paul.
"But we don't want them to see our faces." pointed out Ted. "Back into the nightshirts."

The boys slipped their disguises back on. By now Bert and Harry had got quite a distance from the work-camp and Bert reached the clearing ahead of his friend.

"Wait for me Bert." puffed Harry.
Bert stopped to wait for his friend thinking he was safe from the dreaded phantoms for the moment. He sat on a fallen tree trunk to wait for Harry to catch him up. Harry staggered into the clearing and saw his friend sitting on the tree trunk. That was not all he saw. He skidded to a halt and stood with a look of horror on his face. There, sitting next to his friend was....a lion.

Bert hadn't noticed it as he was still trying to catch his breath.

"Bert." hissed Harry, trying not to startle the lion.
"What is it?" gasped Bert still struggling for breath.
"Don't look now." hissed Harry, "but you're sitting next to a lion."
"You're pulling my leg." said Bert.
"It's the lion that will be pulling your leg in a minute." he warned his friend.

As he was saying this, Harry was backing away slowly from Bert and the lion. It was at this moment that Bert noticed a snake slithering across the grass towards his friend.

"Harry." he called across to his friend.
"What?" asked Harry, still backing away from
Bert.
"There's a snake by your foot." whispered Bert.

It was at the same moment that Bert spotted
Louis that Harry spotted Samantha. With yells of
terror, the two men were off again, charging
back towards the work-camp and the awaiting
phantoms. The boys had heard the yell of panic
and had guessed the two workmen had met
their animal friends.

"Get ready." warned Ted. "I think we're going to
have visitors."

A moment later the two unfortunate figures
came charging back into the work-camp, straight
towards the three phantoms who began wailing
and moaning again.

It was all too much for poor old Bert and Harry.
With another yell of terror, the two workmen
shot off through the woods in the direction of the
village as fast as their legs would carry them,
leaving behind the three phantoms helpless with
laughter.
"That was the funniest thing I've ever seen."

choked Ted.

"They didn't half move." laughed Paul.

I think we'd better move and collect the animals." pointed out Peter.

"Just a minute." said Ted. "I've got to write a note."

"Who on earth are you going to write to?" asked Paul.

"Bert and Harry are expecting the driver of the bulldozer to arrive and start knocking down the trees," explained Ted.

"So?" said Peter, not understanding what Ted was getting at.

"Perhaps a note will stop him doing it." said Ted.

"What are you going to write?" asked Paul.

Ted took out a piece of paper and a pen from his pocket and began to write the message. It read, "Work cancelled until further notice."

Ted signed it Bert and Harry, then climbed onto the bulldozer and put the note on the window where it would be easily seen. That done, he climbed down again, and the three boys set off to find the animals. They found them without any trouble, and they made their way back to Sleepy Hollow to report to Mrs. Muldoon.

As they made their way through the woods,

Tom, the bulldozer driver arrived at the work-camp. He was rather surprised to find no one else there but decided he would start work anyway. It was when he was climbing into his cab that he spotted the note on the window. He collected it and read it.

"That's strange." he thought to himself. "It's not like the council to stop work for no reason. Not that it worries me though." he thought. "I can go fishing."

He climbed back out of his cab, locked the door, and made his way home, to collect his fishing rods. As he approached the telephone kiosk in the village, he thought he had better ring the office to tell them he was going fishing and that he would ring the office the next morning to see if he would be needed then.

Mrs. Osborne answered the phone and took the message, promising to pass it on to Mr. James when he came out of the meeting he was in.

As she put down the phone, into the office staggered Bert and Harry having run all the way from the work-camp. They were so out of breath; they could hardly speak.

"We….we….we…." gasped Bert.

"Want….want….want…." puffed Harry.

"To….to….to…." gasped Bert.

"See….see….see…." spluttered Harry.

"Mr….Mr….Mr….gasped Bert.

"James….James….James…." gulped Harry.

"I'm afraid he's in a meeting at the moment." replied Mrs. Osbourne, not knowing what to make of the two workmen. "Would you like to take a seat and wait?"

Bert and Harry were only too pleased to take a seat and wait. It would give them the chance to get their breath back. They took a seat and waited.

It was not until half-an-hour later that Mr. James came out of his meeting and walked into the office. He saw Bert and Harry sitting there and recognised them as the two men that should have been working at the work-camp.

"What are you two doing here?" he demanded.

"Oh, Mr. James." Bert began. "It was horrible."

"There were no heads." interrupted Harry.

"They went, 'Oooooh, Oooooh'," continued Bert.

"And the lion was…." started Harry, only to be interrupted by Mr. James.

"Just a minute." he snapped at the two workmen.

"What are you babbling on about?"

"We've seen them." whispered Bert.

"Seen who?" asked Mr. James, also whispering.

"Them!" whispered Harry.

"Who are them…I mean who are they?" asked Mr. James getting angry.

"The Headless Phantoms." whispered Bert.

"The what?" demanded Mr. James.

"The Headless Phantoms." repeated Bert.

"All headless they were." added Harry.

"And wailing and groaning." continued Bert.

"Have you two gone stark raving mad?" asked Mr. James.

"No guv'nor." said Bert. "It's the truth."

"They were horrible," said Harry. "They chased us."

"Why did they chase you?" asked Mr. James, still not believing a word of it.

"Because of the curse." explained Harry.

"What curse?" asked his boss.

"The one that says they'll come after you if you damage the wood and Sleepy Hollow." Bert told him.

"Nonsense." snapped Mr. James.

"Don't forget the lion." added Harry.

"What lion?" asked Mr. James.

"It was in the wood with the snake." Bert told him.

"That's part of the curse too." said Harry.

"I don't know about lions, but I think you two are
lying."

"We're not lying." said Bert angrily.

"Who told you about the curse?" asked Mr.
James.

"Three boys we met in the wood." explained
Harry.

"Three boys?" asked Mr. James suspiciously.
"Describe these three boys to me."

Bert and Harry went on to describe Ted, Paul,
and Peter.

"You have been tricked you idiots!" stormed Mr.
James. "There are no Headless Phantoms."

"But we saw them." insisted Harry.

"How many boys were there?" asked Mr. James.

"Three." replied Bert.

"And how many so-called Headless Phantoms
were there?" asked Mr. James.

"Three." said Bert, "But what has that......?"

He stopped mid-sentence. He was beginning to
see what his boss was getting at. The Phantoms
were nothing more than three boys dressed up.

"Why the little perishers." shouted Bert. "Wait til I
get my hands on them. They'll be real Phantoms

by the time I've finished with them!"

"But how do you explain the lion and the snake?" asked Harry. "We both saw them."

"I can't explain it at the moment." admitted Mr. James. "But I bet those three had something to do with it."

"What do we do now boss?" asked Bert.

"Get back to the work-camp and start work, the bulldozer driver will be wondering where you are."

Mrs. Osbourne, who had been watching the strange proceedings going on in her office remembered the telephone message she had received.

"Excuse me Mr. James." she interrupted. "I had a message from the bulldozer driver while you were in a meeting."

"What did he want?" asked Mr. James.

"He said that he got the note and as there was no work to be done today, he was going fishing." Mrs. Osbourne told him.

"What note?" asked Mr. James. "I didn't leave him a note."

"Neither did we." explained Harry. "We had no time to write a note. We left in rather a hurry."

"I bet it was those three boys." fumed Mr. James.

"Calm down sir." said a concerned Mrs. Osbourne. "You've gone all red."

"Had we better get back to the site?" asked Bert.

"There's no point." said Mr. James angrily. "You can't do much without a bulldozer."

"What shall we do then?" asked Harry.

"You'd better report to the foreman and get him to find you some jobs in the yard." said Mr. James.

"Yes sir." said Bert and Harry together as they turned to leave.

"Make sure you're at the work-camp early tomorrow." ordered Mr. James.

"Why sir?" asked Bert.

"Because I'll be there as well." said Mr. James. "We're going to start by knocking down that old woman's house. Once we've done that, those pesky kids will have nothing more to demonstrate about and will leave us to get on with the rest of the job."

CHAPTER 8

PREPARING FOR BATTLE

While all of the commotion had been going on down at the Council Offices, Ted, Paul, and Peter had been enjoying a big dinner that Mrs. Muldoon had prepared for them. They were now talking over plans for the coming battle they expected with the council.

"I don't think we have anything to worry about until tomorrow morning." said Ted.
"I agree." said Paul. "Leaving that note on the bulldozer was a good idea. It's given us some breathing space to get things organised."
"Does that mean we can have a rest?" asked Peter.
"No chance." said Ted. "We must use all the time we have to prepare for the next part of my plan."
"What do you think they'll do next?" asked Paul.
"I think they'll come to the house and try to get us out." said Ted.
"What are we going to do if they do that?" asked a worried Peter.
"We'll need some weapons." announced Ted.
"Do you mean guns and things?" asked Peter.
"Of course not." chuckled Ted. "We can't go

around shooting the council, they won't like it!"
"What kind of weapons do you mean then?"
asked Paul.
"Well, there's Louis and Samantha for a start."
replied Ted.
"They're animals not weapons." pointed out
Peter.
"But we can use them to frighten the enemy like
we did with Bert and Harry." explained Ted.
"That's true." said Paul. "But we will need more
than those two if we are to hold up the council."
"I know said Ted, the problem is, what can we
use?"
"Can I make a suggestion?" asked Mrs. Muldoon.
"Of course." said Ted. "We need all the help we
can get."
"We could make some bombs." suggested Mrs.
Muldoon.
"Bombs!" exclaimed Paul.
"Not real one's silly boy." laughed Mrs. Muldoon.
"I mean flour bombs and the like."
"What on earth are flour bombs?" asked Peter.
"You get some paper bags," explained Mrs.
Muldoon, "fill them with flour and fire them at the
enemy. When they hit them, the bags will burst,
and the flour goes all over them."
"I like it, I like it," said Ted enthusiastically.
"We must protect the house." pointed out Paul. "If

they get in, we've lost the battle."
"We can lock the shutters on all the windows and lock and bolt all the doors." said Mrs. Muldoon.
"We'd better make a start." suggested Peter. "We've got a lot to do."
"Come down to the cellar," said Mrs. Muldoon. "I think you'll find all you need there."

She led the way into the entrance hall and towards the door under the stairs. She unlocked it and switched on a light that lit up the stairs leading to the cellar. She led the way down the stone steps leading to a darkened room below. The boys shivered. They were not sure if it was because it was much colder down in the cellar or because it was a little spooky. At the bottom of the steps Mrs. Muldoon pressed another switch on the wall and the cellar was illuminated by a number of lights which were hung at different points from the ceiling of the cellar.

The cellar itself seemed enormous to the boys as they wandered about exploring the room. It was an interesting place with lots of strange things to see. In the corner, they found a pile of old sacks and hundreds of bottles. In another there stood a huge cupboard which when opened revealed every possible tool the boys could think of. The third corner contained barrels of a dark, sticky liquid which Mrs. Muldoon explained was left over from when the garden shed was painted. In the last corner was a large table which Mrs. Muldoon said they could use as a worktable.

A wicked grin appeared on Ted's face.

"I've just had a brilliant idea." he announced.
"Not another one." groaned Paul.
"Wait until you hear it." Ted replied. "Then you can decide how good it is."
"Go on then," said Paul, "let's hear it."
"We use the barrels of tar as an extra way to defend the house." Ted told him.
"How can barrels of tar help us?" asked Peter.
"If we take the old tin bath from the cellar, balance it on the edge above the front door, fill it with tar......"

Ted did not have to explain any further, judging by the huge grins on Paul and Peters faces they knew exactly what would happen.
"Surely you don't intend to tip it over the council workmen?" said Mrs. Muldoon, trying to sound shocked and keep herself from smiling.
"I do." chuckled Ted.

"But that would be very naughty." she told him as a huge grin appeared on her face.

"It would." admitted Ted. "But it would also be a lot of fun as well."

"Not for the council workmen it wouldn't." Peter told him.

"I have to say that's one of your better ideas Ted." Paul told his brother.

"Am I not brilliant?" boasted Ted.

"I wouldn't go that far!" Paul told him.

"We'd better start with the flour bombs." said Paul.

"Where's the flour?" asked Peter.

"I haven't got any flour," said Mrs. Muldoon.

"How can we make flour bombs without flour?" asked Ted.

"I may not have any flour." said Mrs. Muldoon, "but in those sacks I think you will find something just as good."

The boys went to investigate the sacks. On opening one of them, they found it to be full of white powder.

"What is it?" asked Peter.

"It's plaster." explained Mrs. Muldoon.

"If you don't mix it with water, it'll be just like flour."

"Sounds just the job." said Paul, "Let's get on with

it."

Between them, the three boys between them
managed to drag the heavy bag across to the
table they were going to use as a workbench.
Mrs. Muldoon went to the cupboard where the
tools were and from a draw in the bottom of it
collected dozens and dozens of paper bags and
a large ball of string. She left the boys to their
jobs and went to prepare some refreshments for
later.

The boys set up a production line. Peter opened
the bags and passed them to Ted who used a
scoop to fill them with the plaster powder from
the sack. Then he passed the full bags on to Paul
who tied up the bags with string. They changed
jobs occasionally to stop them getting bored
with doing the same thing. An hour later, Mrs.
Muldoon came back down the cellar steps with a
tray of pop and sandwiches, to find the boys had
made one hundred and ten plaster bombs.

"My, you have been busy." Mrs. Muldoon
complimented them on their achievement.
"Well, it will do for a start." said Ted.
"You mean we've got more to do?" groaned
Peter.
"Not now, you haven't." said Mrs. Muldoon. "It's

time for a break and some refreshments."
The boys were not going to argue, and they
tucked into the food and drink like starving
wolves.

"What have we got to do next?" asked Peter, as
they finished their food.
"I think we should decide how we are going to
protect the house." suggested Paul.
"That's a good idea." agreed Ted. "Clearly we
can't protect every part of it, there's not enough
of us."
"I agree," said Peter. "I think the best place for us
to take up our positions is on the landing upstairs.
From there we can look out over the garden and
see anyone approaching the front door."
"That's good thinking." Ted complimented his
friend. "We could also launch the plaster bombs
from there."
"What's that?" asked Paul, noticing a pile of
plastic tubing in one corner of the cellar.
"Oh, that's the old hose pipe we used to water
the garden with." explained Mrs. Muldoon. "It's no
good now, there are holes in it and the water just
sprays out everywhere."
"That might be just what we need." said Peter.
"How can an old hose full of holes be any use to
us?" asked Ted with a puzzled look on his face.

"Let's take it out into the garden and I'll show you." said Peter.

While Ted and Peter carried the old hosepipe up from the cellar and out into the garden, Paul and Mrs. Muldoon began loading the plaster bombs into trays to carry them upstairs to the landing. When they reached the landing, they watched as Ted and Peter unrolled the hosepipe and laid it down the side of the garden path.

"I wonder what they're up to?" thought Paul.

As he watched them, he looked around the rest of the garden. They had been right to choose this as their vantage point. Paul could see the whole garden and the path leading up to the front door. Ted and Peter came back into the house. "What have you two been up to?" he asked them. "We'll show you." smiled Peter mysteriously.

He went to the top of the stairs and called down to Mrs. Muldoon who was in the kitchen below.

"Tap 1." he yelled.

Down in the kitchen, Mrs. Muldoon turned on the kitchen tap. In a matter of seconds, the water was shooting out of the holes in the hosepipe and high into the air to fall down again over the garden path, Ted having blocked the end of the hosepipe to stop the water shooting out of the end.

"That'll do." called Ted.
"Off Tap 1." the instruction was called down to the kitchen where the tap was turned off.
"That's great." said Paul.
"That's not all." said Ted as he nodded to Peter. "Watch this."

"Tap 2." Peter called down to Mrs. Muldoon.

Down in the kitchen the second tap was turned on. This time a jet of water shot out of the end of the second hosepipe that was sticking out of the landing window aimed at the garden path below. This pipe was not damaged, and the water shot out of the end of it and down on to the path below. The hosepipe could be aimed at anyone walking up the path to the front door.

"Off 2."called out Peter and the water stopped shooting out of the pipe as Mrs. Muldoon turned off the tap in the kitchen below.
"Let's go over the plan." said Ted. "First, we use

the hosepipe along the garden path, that should soak them. Next, we use the hosepipe through the window to soak them even more. Then we use the plaster bombs, then the bath of tar balanced on the ledge over the front door and if all else fails we let the animals loose."

"I can see one problem." said Peter.

"What's that?" asked Ted.

"It's the plaster bombs." continued Peter. "We can only use them when they are close to the house so we can hit them. We won't be able to throw them very far."

"That's a good point." conceded Ted. "Anyone have any ideas on how we can solve this problem?"

"I think I can help," volunteered Mrs. Muldoon. "Down in the cellar there are some long strips of elastic. It should be quite easy to rig up some sort of catapult to use to launch the plaster bombs."

"I'll fetch it." said Peter running downstairs.

"Bring a hammer and some nails." Mrs. Muldoon called down after him.

"Why do we need hammer and nails?" asked Ted.

"If we stretch the elastic across the open landing window." Mrs. Muldoon explained, "nail the ends each side of the window, it should make an effective catapult and increase the range of the plaster bombs."

Peter returned with the elastic, hammer, and nails and the boys proceeded to set up the catapult. The elastic was stretched across the open window and held firmly while Paul nailed each end into the window frame. Mrs. Muldoon didn't seem to mind that they were hammering nails into her woodwork. It only took a matter of minutes before the job was done.

"We'd better test it to see if it works." said Ted.

He got a bag of plaster from the pile and placed it in the centre of the elastic and then slowly began to pull the elastic back. It was stretched quite a long way. Then he released it and they all watched as the plaster bomb shot through the window, at what seemed an incredible speed to land halfway down the garden path where it burst sending the plaster powder into the air in a cloud.

"Wow!" said Ted, "That's better than I thought was possible."

"Give me a go." said Paul, eager to see what he could do.

"No." argued Ted. "We can't afford to waste our

ammunition."
Paul could see the sense of this so did not
pursue the matter.

"Come on." said Peter. "Let's get that old tin bath
up from the cellar and balanced on the ledge
over the front door. Then we can get it filled with
the tar."

Back down to the cellar they went and while Ted
and Paul carried the old bath up to the landing,
Peter got a bucket and collected some of the tar
from one of the barrels. Whilst he was doing this,
Dilys, who had somehow managed to get down
into the cellar, was edging nearer to the barrels.
Luckily, Peter spotted her before she could dip
her head in the tar.

"Get out of it, Dilys." he scolded her, pushing her
away.

Mrs. Muldoon appeared and led away a very
reluctant donkey. Peter went upstairs with the
bucket of tar.
"That daft donkey is trying to drink this stuff." he
told the other two.
"Trust Dilys." laughed Ted.
"She loves the taste of it." said Mrs. Muldoon. "As

fast as we used to paint the shed, she'd be licking it off again."

They had to make several journeys down to the cellar with the bucket until they had the bath three quarters full of tar.

Dilys found her way upstairs and before they knew it, she had her head out of the window lapping at the tar in the bath, nearly tipping it over. They managed to drag her away from it before she did any damage.

"I'm glad we've finished." puffed Ted when they had at last made all the preparations they could.

The rest of the evening was spent relaxing and getting ready for the battle that was to start tomorrow. Each of the boys were a little bit nervous about what might happen tomorrow They didn't know what to expect; all they knew was they had to do everything in their power to help Mrs. Muldoon keep her home.

CHAPTER 9

INTO BATTLE

The following morning the boys were up early making final preparations for the battle to come. After checking Dilys had not got at the bath of tar and drunk it all, they sat down to wait for the enemy. The time passed very slowly, and the boys were getting impatient.

"I wish they'd get a move on." complained Ted.
"Why don't they come?" moaned Peter.
"I can't stand all this hanging about." added Paul.
"I don't think you'll see anyone until after nine o'clock." Mrs. Muldoon told them. "The offices don't open until nine."
"That means another hour to wait." groaned Paul.
"Why don't you go out on a scouting party to the work-camp?" suggested Mrs. Muldoon. "You could find out how many of them there are."
"Good idea." said Ted. "We'll take Louis for a walk."

Dilys wanted to go as well but they managed to get out of the house without her noticing. With Louis on the lead, they made their way to the work-camp and took up a hiding place behind

106

some bushes. Bert and Harry were waiting there nervously.

Tom the bulldozer driver arrived.

"Where did you get to yesterday?" Bert asked him.

"As there was no work, I went fishing." explained Tom.

"That note was a fake." Harry informed him.

"Well, I wasn't to know that." said Tom. "And anyway, if there was work, where were you two?"

"We were chased away by the Headless Phantoms." explained Bert.

"The what?" asked Tom.

"And a lion and a snake." added Harry.

"Headless Phantoms? Lions? Snakes? Have you been drinking?" asked Tom.

"It's true." insisted Bert. "They chased us away."

"We reported the matter to Mr. James." continued Harry.

"And he's coming here this morning to sort it out." Bert added.

"What?" said Tom. "The boss coming here. We'd better start work."

Tom went over to his machine, unlocked it, and climbed into the cab. He started the engine and it roared into life. It was not the only thing to roar into life. Louis, frightened by the noise of the engine let out a roar and pulled free from Ted. He leapt out of bushes into the clearing. Bert and Harry fell to the floor in terror. Tom couldn't believe his eyes. There was a lion bounding towards him. He quickly locked himself in the cab, but unfortunately knocked the machine onto reverse gear. It started moving backwards towards a car arriving at the work-camp. The car was being driven by Mr. James.

Seeing the bulldozer chugging towards him, Mr. James had to take avoiding action. He swerved the car, but unfortunately, he swerved it into a ditch.

By now, Louis had disappeared into the wood and was heading back towards Sleepy Hollow. Bert and Harry were still lying face down on the ground afraid to look up in case the lion was still there. Tom had got out of the bulldozer, and making sure there was no sign of the lion, had rushed to help a rather shaken Mr. James out of his car.

"Mr. James are you alright?" asked the concerned workman.

"I think so." said Mr. James. "But no thanks to you. What on earth are you playing at?"

"It was a lion…" began Tom.

"Now don't you start." snapped his boss, "I had enough of that yesterday with those other two idiots. Where are they by the way?"

Both men looked across the clearing to where the two workmen still lay face down on the ground.

"What on earth are they playing at?" asked Mr. James. "What are you doing?" he asked them, walking over towards them, followed by Tom who was still keeping a look out in case the lion reappeared.
"It was the lion." began Harry, getting up.
"I didn't see any lion." snapped Mr. James.
"We did." chorused the three workmen.
"Well, it's not here now." said their boss. "Now come and give me a hand to get my car out of the ditch."

The four men walked over to the ditch. Luckily, it wasn't too deep, and the car did not seem badly damaged. It proved quite easy to get the car out. Mr. James locked it and then turned to speak to his workmen.

"Now we'll get over to Sleepy Hollow and get that old woman out of her house. She's caused us enough trouble already. At least with those kids out of the way we should have no trouble in getting her out."

"That's what he thinks." said Ted to the other two from their hiding place behind the bushes.

"Come on." said Paul. "If we take the short-cut, we can be at Sleepy Hollow before them.

"What about Louis?" asked Peter.

"I expect he's already back there." said Ted as the three boys raced back to Sleepy Hollow using the short-cut.

Louis was indeed back at Sleepy Hollow and when the boys arrived, he was having a bowl of milk. The boys had only just begun to tell Mrs. Muldoon of what happened when the enemy arrived.

"They're here!" announced Peter looking through the window.

The four men entered the garden and began walking up the path towards the house. Mrs. Muldoon went out onto the front doorstep. The boys stayed indoors out of sight.

"What do you want?" Mrs. Muldoon demanded as they walked towards her.

"Just to talk to you." replied Mr. James as they continued to walk up the path.

"Get out of my garden." ordered Mrs. Muldoon.

"Come now, Mrs. Muldoon, I only want to…." continued Mr. James.

"Don't come any nearer." warned the old lady.

The workmen were now half-way down the path and had just passed the end of the hosepipe that had been placed alongside the path. Mrs. Muldoon went back inside the house, locking and bolting the door behind her. The enemy continued to advance.

Inside the house, instructions were given.

"Tap 1." yelled Ted to Peter.

In the kitchen, Peter turned on the kitchen tap. The water shot through it, and reaching the holes in the pipe in the garden, began shooting up into the air and cascading down over the advancing workmen.

"What's happening?" spluttered Mr. James.

"It's started to rain." suggested Harry.

"It can't be rain, Harry." said Bert.

"Why not?" asked Harry.

"Well, it's only raining on the path." pointed out

Bert. "The rest of the garden is dry."
"It's coming out of the holes in that hosepipe you idiots." spluttered Mr. James. "Quick, back to the gate."

The men ran back to the gate and out of range of the water.

"Off tap 1." ordered Ted as he watched them retreat.
Peter turned off the water. Back at the garden gate stood four soggy men and one of them was absolutely furious.

"It must be those perishing kids." fumed Mr. James. "If I ever get my hands on them...."
"What are we going to do now?" asked Tom.
"Simple." said Mr. James. "Bert and Harry will take this knife and go and cut that hosepipe as near to the house as they can get."
"But we'll get wet." protested Bert.
"You're already wet." pointed out Mr. James, giving him the knife.
"He's right Bert." said Harry. "We are already wet."
"Oh, get on with it you fools." shouted Mr. James.

Bert and Harry began walking down the path towards the house. As soon as they reached the hosepipe, the water was turned on again and once more the water cascaded down over the unfortunate men.

"I wish I'd learned to swim." moaned Harry.
"I think I'm drowning." complained Bert.
"We should have brought umbrellas." pointed out Harry.
"I'm sure to catch a cold after this." said Bert.

By now, the two men had reached the downstairs window through which the hosepipe had been pushed. Using the knife they cut the pipe at the window ledge and tramped back up the garden path to the gate. Ted, seeing what they had done, ordered the water to be turned off. Back at the gate Mr. James seemed to be in a better mood.

"Well done men." he congratulated a dripping Bert and Harry.

Back in the house, changes were being made to Ted's original plan.

"Well, they've destroyed our first weapon." said Paul.
"Not quite." said Ted. "I think we can still make

use of the hosepipe."

"How?" asked Peter.

"I'll tell you in a minute." said Ted. "When they next come up the path, we'll use the hosepipe from the upstairs window."

"But what about this hosepipe?" asked Peter.

"Bert and Harry did us a favour when they cut off the damaged part." began Ted.

"We can still use the part that is inside the house that's not damaged."

"But how do we use it?" asked Peter.

"We re-position the hosepipe behind the letterbox of the front door." explained Ted.

"I'm beginning to understand." chuckled Paul.

"Oh, you're not going to......" began Mrs. Muldoon.

"We are." said the three boys together.

The hosepipe was quickly positioned behind the letterbox and the boys raced back up to the landing to keep watch on the enemy. No sooner were they in position, the workmen began to advance down the path towards the house. Mr. James was confident that they were quite safe this time. He was about to be proved wrong.

"Tap 2." Ted called down to Mrs. Muldoon.

Down in the kitchen she turned on the second

tap while Ted pointed the hosepipe at Mr. James. The water shot out with such a force that it knocked Mr. James off his feet.

He slithered about in the mud that was once the garden path, trying to get to his feet. Bert and Harry found this amusing and began laughing.

They didn't laugh for long however, as Ted directed the hosepipe at them, and they too were knocked off their feet and ended up slithering in the mud with Mr. James. Tom had already made a hasty retreat back to the safety of the garden gate.

"Quick." Mr. James ordered Bert and Harry. "If we can get under the ledge over the front door, they won't be able to hit us with the water."

Half walking, half crawling the three men made it to the safety of the front door.

"Off tap 2." called out Ted, and the water was turned off.

Inside the house the boys quietly made their way downstairs and joined Mrs. Muldoon behind the front door. Mr. James hammered on the front door from the outside.

"What do you want?" asked Mrs. Muldoon.

"If you don't surrender, I will lose my temper." yelled Mr. James.

"Sounds as if he's already lost it." chuckled Ted.

"I will not surrender." called back Mrs. Muldoon.

"At least come out and talk it over." suggested Mr. James, hoping to trick Mrs. Muldoon into opening the door.

"I'm not unlocking this door." Mrs. Muldoon informed him.

"But we can't talk through a locked door." protested Mr. James.

"If you want to talk to me, you can do it through the letter-box." called out Mrs. Muldoon, trying not to laugh.

Mr. James was very annoyed that his plan had not worked. He knelt down in front of the letterbox and pushed it open.

"Now, Mrs. Muldoon......" he began.

He didn't get any further. Ted had quietly told Peter to turn on the tap in the kitchen. One moment, Mr. James was speaking, the next he was almost drowning as the water shot through the letterbox into his face. He went tumbling backwards into Bert and Harry, and all three tumbled backwards onto the muddy garden path. Ted continued to direct the water through the letterbox until the three men had scrambled back to the gate.

"Enemy defeated." announced Ted. "Water off." "I don't think Mr. James will give up that easily." Mrs. Muldoon told them. "I think he'll be back." "If he comes back, we'll be ready for him." announced Ted confidently.

CHAPTER 10

SABOTAGE

If Ted could have heard Mr. James at that moment, he would not have sounded so confident. The Deputy Clerk of the council was furious. Bert, Harry, and Tom had never seen anyone so angry. He led them back through the woods to the work-camp.

"Just wait!" stormed Mr. James. "They'll be in trouble for this."
"What are you going to do boss?" asked Harry.
"I'm going to stop their interfering." snapped Mr. James.

Going over to his car, he took out the two-way radio he always carried. This connected him with the office.

"Mrs. Osbourne, I want you to contact the Water Board and get them to turn off the water supply to Sleepy Hollow. Is that clear?"
"Perfectly, sir." came back the secretary's voice over the radio.
"I also want you to call the police and tell them to send an officer to Sleepy Hollow where an old

lady and three children are attacking members of the council and stopping them doing their work. Have you got that?" he asked.

"Yes sir." replied Mrs. Osbourne. "I'll do it straight away."

Mr. James returned the radio to his car. Bert, Tom, and Harry had been trying to wring out their clothes.

"Come on, there's no time for that." ordered Mr. James. "Let's get back to Sleepy Hollow."

Muttering under their breath, Bert, Harry, and Tom struggled back into their socks and shoes and followed their leader back to the house.

Back at the house, Mrs. Muldoon had been busy getting some food for the defenders while the enemy were away. The boys had stayed on guard up on the landing to make sure the enemy did not try and sneak back and attack. Mrs. Muldoon brought the squash and sandwiches up to them. It was not until Peter went back down to the kitchen to make some more squash that they discovered that the water had been turned off. He raced back upstairs to tell them the news.

"We've got a problem." he announced."
"What?" asked Ted.
"They've turned the water off." he told them.
"I was afraid something like this might happen."
said Ted.
"What are we going to do now?" asked Paul.
"Use the plaster bombs." said Ted. "When they
come back, they won't be expecting another
attack.
"You won't have to wait long." Mrs. Muldoon told
them, looking out of the window. "They're back!"

The boys sprang into action. Ted opened the
window, Paul put the first bag of plaster into the
sling and Peter pulled it back and waited for the
order to release the bomb. The four men began
walking up the garden path towards the house.

"Why don't you turn on the water?" called out Mr.
James.

He got no reply.

"What a pity." laughed Mr. James. "They seem to
have run out of water.

The other three men joined in the laughter. They
were not laughing for long.

"Fire!" yelled Ted.

"Where?" asked Bert.

"We've got no water to put it out." wailed Harry.

It didn't take them long to realise that the "fire" was not a fire but the order for Peter to release the first plaster bomb. Peter released the elastic, and the first bomb went sailing through the air towards its intended target. It was right on target. It hit Mr. James on the head and burst covering him in white powder which at once began to stick to his wet clothes.

"Fire 2." yelled Ted.

The second missile was released and went hurtling towards its target. This one hit Harry on the head with similar results to the first.

"Fire at will." called out Ted.

"Who's Will?" asked Bert as the bag burst on his chest making him cough and splutter.

'Fire at will' of course meant fire at any time and at anyone. Peter didn't need telling twice. As fast as Paul could load the catapults, Peter found a target to aim at. Some were hits, others misses, bursting on the path. Some twenty to thirty bombs had been fired before the unfortunate council workers once more retreated to the safety of the gate, out of range of the plaster bombs.

They looked a mess, covered with plaster which had begun to set hard on their wet clothes. Bert had so much plaster covering him he looked more like a snowman than a council workman.

"What do we do now?" asked Harry, trying to remove bits of plaster from his hair.
"Well, I'm going home for a hot bath." announced Bert.
"Me too." added Tom.
"No!" shouted Mr. James. "I will not be beaten by three kids and an old woman. We'll try one more attack, but this time we'll split up and move about to dodge those bags."

The other three reluctantly agreed to one more charge and set off running towards the house, spreading out as they went.

"Trouble." warned Peter, watching from the landing window.
"What now?" asked Ted.
"They're separating and coming in from different

directions." Peter told him.

"What'll we do?" asked Mrs. Muldoon.

"Keep firing the bombs so they think we're still here." said Ted.

"What are you going to do?" asked Paul.

"I'm going to open the downstairs window." Ted told his brother.

"Have you gone mad?" asked Paul. "They'll get into the house."

"That's what I'm counting on." replied Ted. "Louis will be waiting for them."

"I like it, I like it." smiled Mrs. Muldoon, rubbing her hands.

While they had been talking, Dilys had appeared on the landing. She was fed up with everyone ignoring her. She wanted some company, but most of all, she wanted some of that tar which she could smell in the bath on the ledge above the door. Luckily, Mrs. Muldoon spotted her before she had a chance to get to the bath and managed to pull her back.

"If we're not careful, she'll tip the bath over." warned the old lady.

Mrs. Muldoon led a rather bad-tempered donkey back downstairs while Peter and Paul continued to fire the plaster bombs at the enemy.

Ted dashed downstairs to the library where Louis had been kept with his lead tied to a chair next to the window. He proceeded to open the window. This done, he left the library, closing the door behind him.

The four men managed to reach the wall of the house without being hit by anymore plaster bombs and it was Mr. James who found the open library window.

"Over here." he whispered to the others. "I've found an open window."

The other three edged all along the wall to join Mr. James. He stood with his back to the window, watching them get nearer and nearer.

"Now this is what we'll do..." he told them. "We'll...." He stopped talking because the other three men were behaving strangely. They were backing away from him.

"Where are you going?" he demanded.
"Th....th....th....th...." spluttered Bert.
"B....b....b....b....behind..." stammered Harry.
"Now don't tell me there's one of your Headless Phantoms behind me." sneered Mr. James.

"No, it's not one of them." said Tom.

"Well, what is the matter then?" asked Mr. James.

"You're not going to believe this." said Bert.

"Not going to believe what?" snapped Mr. James.

"There's a lion behind you." said Bert.

"Don't be so si......" began Mr. James, turning around to look in the window.

He found himself staring into the face of Louis. With a yell of terror he turned and ran as fast as he could after Bert, Harry, and Tom who were already halfway down the path. Mr. James soon caught them up and passed them heading for the gate.

Through the gate he ran and risked a glance behind him to make sure the lion wasn't following. Not looking where he was going, he ran straight into the policeman who was arriving in response to his request. Both of them went sprawling to the floor with the other three workmen narrowly missing them.

"I'm very sorry constable." apologised Mr. James, helping the policeman to his feet.

"It's a serious offence to assault a police-officer sir." puffed the constable.

"I'm sorry, it was an accident." said Mr. James.

"You should be more careful." advised the

policeman. "Why were you in such a hurry?"

"I was being chased by a lion." Mr. James informed him.

"I beg your pardon?" said the policeman. "You did say a lion, didn't you?

"Of course I said a lion." snapped Mr. James.

"You wouldn't be trying to be funny would you sir?" asked the policeman.

"I'm quite serious." insisted Mr. James.

"I see." said the policeman. "Have you been drinking sir?"

"How dare you!" yelled Mr. James. "I'm telling you I was chased by a lion."

"Of course." said the policeman taking out his notebook and writing in it. "I was chased by a lion." he wrote.

"What's your name sir?" the policeman asked him.

"I'm Mr. Arthur James, Deputy Clerk of the local council." said Mr. James importantly.

"If you don't mind me saying sir," said the policeman. "You don't look much like a Deputy Clerk covered in all that white stuff."

"I was attacked by three hooligans and an old lady." replied Mr. James.

The policeman wrote this down in his notebook and then proceeded to take a statement from Bert, Harry, and Tom, after which he was more confused than ever. They all seemed mad to him.

Any further questioning had to wait as someone else was coming towards them, not from the direction of the house, but the village. Mr. James recognised the figure at once. It was Mr. Thompson, the Clerk of the council. Mr. Thompson on the other hand did not recognise his Deputy which was hardly surprising the state Mr. James was in.

"Mr. Thompson." began Mr. James. "I wasn't expecting you until tomorrow."

The Clerk looked at the figure who had just spoken to him and then spoke to the policeman.

"Who is this scruffy looking person?" he asked.
"Says he's Mr. James, Deputy Clerk of the council." replied the policeman.
"Arthur?" said the Clerk, looking closely at the figure before him. "Is that you?"
"Yes sir." replied the unfortunate Deputy Clerk.
"What on earth happened to you?" asked the Clerk.
"I have been attacked by three hooligans and an old lady." explained Mr. James. "They have held up the work on the by-pass, we haven't even

started work yet."

"Excellent!" said the Clerk.

"I beg your pardon?" said a puzzled Mr. James.

"I said excellent." repeated the Clerk.

"But....but....but...." spluttered Mr. James.

"I have received a letter from a Mr. Thomas which, to put simply means we are going to change the route of the by-pass."

"What!" yelled Mr. James. "Do you mean I've gone through all this for nothing?"

"Not at all Arthur." said the Clerk. "I'm very pleased you have not started work."

"I want those three hooligans punished." demanded Mr. James.

"Punished, Arthur?" said the Clerk. "Certainly not. By holding up the work, those hooligans as you call them have saved us thousands of pounds."

"But....but....but...." spluttered Mr. James.

"Come on Arthur. Let's go and meet these hooligans of yours." said the Clerk.

The Clerk led the way up the garden path towards the house, followed by his very unhappy Deputy, the three workmen, and the policeman. From the landing window the defenders watched their advance.

"Here they come again." warned Mrs. Muldoon.

"We're ready for them." said Ted.

"They've got reinforcements." said Paul.
"And one of them is a policeman." pointed out Peter.

As the men approached the house, Mr. Thompson called out to the house.

"Mrs. Muldoon. I'm Mr. Thompson, the Clerk of the council."
"What do you want?" called back Mrs. Muldoon.
"I want to tell you that your house is safe. We are not going to knock it down and the by-pass is going to be built on the other side of the village." the Clerk informed her.
"Don't believe him." yelled Ted. "It's just a trick to get us to open the door and let them in."
"It's not a trick, I promise you." called back the Clerk.
"And if you don't believe me, this policeman will make sure nobody enters your house unless you give your permission."

The policeman confirmed that he would do just that and Mrs. Muldoon agreed to go down and speak to them. The boys decided they had better put Louis and Samantha down in the cellar for now to avoid any awkward questions being asked about them. This done, the boys went to the front door with Mrs. Muldoon. She unlocked it and they all went out on the front doorstep.

"We'll stay here." said Ted. "Just in case they try and trick us."

Leaving the boys to guard the door, Mrs. Muldoon went down the path to meet the advancing men.

The boys waited on the front doorstep, ever alert in case a surprise attack came. They watched the adults wishing they could hear what was being said. Mr. Thompson was deep in conversation with Mrs. Muldoon, and she seemed to be very pleased with what he was saying to her. Suddenly, Mr. Thompson stopped speaking and stared at the house.

"Excuse me, Mrs. Muldoon, but isn't that a donkey sticking its head out of your window?" he asked her.

"Oh," said Mrs. Muldoon. spinning round and looking up at the landing window. "That's Dilys. She's after the bath."

"Dilys? After the bath?" said a puzzled Mr. Thompson.

"She'll tip it over if she's not careful." said Mrs.

Muldoon.

Which is exactly what Dilys did. She had seen the chance to get at the black sticky liquid she loved. Her head edged ever nearer to the bath! She nudged it forward so that it rocked on the edge of the ledge.

"Look out!" yelled Mrs. Muldoon to the three boys standing beneath it.

The warning came too late. The bath rocked and then tilted. Only the string tying it to the ledge prevented the bath itself falling onto the boys below causing a nasty accident. As it was, it was bad enough that the contents of the bath were heading towards the unsuspecting boys below. One minute they were standing there without a care in the world, the next everything went black as the tar covered all three of them from head to toe.

Mr. James shrieked with delight as he saw the three boys get a taste of their own medicine. Bert, Harry, and Tom joined in the hysterical laughter and soon everyone, except the three unfortunate victims were howling with laughter.

"Hee-haw, hee-haw, hee-haw," brayed Dilys.

Even she seemed to be laughing at the boys.
When they looked at each other and the state
they were in, even the boys could see the funny
side of things and joined in the laughter. The
adults walked back to the house to see what
could be done.

"You'd all better have a bath." said Mrs. Muldoon,
to the three boys.
"But you haven't got any water." pointed out
Peter.
"Oh dear." said Mrs. Muldoon. "I'd quite forgotten
about that."
"Don't worry." said Mr. Thompson. "We'll get them
safely home in our council lorries."
"Before you go." said Mrs. Muldoon, "I'd like to
invite you all to a party here at Sleepy Hollow,
tomorrow at three o'clock."
"Even me?" asked Mr. James.
"Even you, Mr. James." replied Mrs. Muldoon.
"And boys, if your parents would like to come,
they would be very welcome."

Leaving Bert and Harry behind to tidy up the
mess, the rest of the group made their way back
to the work-camp. The policeman left in his

police car, Mr. Thompson and Mr. James left in their cars and Tom drove the boys home in the back of one of the council lorries.

CHAPTER 11

A HAPPY ENDING

After dropping Peter off at his house, Tom drove Ted and Paul to their home. He left them on the pavement and drove off. The boys stood for a moment, looking at the house as if plucking up the courage to go in.

"What do you think Mam will say?" asked Paul.
"I don't think she's going to be very pleased." said Ted.

At that moment, the front door opened, and Mrs. Thomas came out. She gave a little scream when she saw the two black figures standing there. She did not recognise them.

"Hello Mam." said Ted.
"We've had a bit of an accident." added Paul.

She gave another scream realising it was her sons and called for her husband to come at once. He arrived on the doorstep alongside his wife and stared at the two creatures.

"Who are they?" he asked his wife.

"I think, 'what are they?' would be a better question." she replied.

"They're our two sons." she added.

"What on earth have you done now?" demanded their father.

Before they could explain further, their mother took control of the situation and ordered them into the back yard where they were made to get out of their ruined clothes.

"Can we go in now?" asked Ted, embarrassed at having to stand in the back yard in only his underpants.

Their mother led both of the boys inside and up to the bathroom where they were told to get themselves cleaned up.

It simply took ages. Luckily, their clothes had prevented their bodies getting stained, but their faces and their hair were a terrible mess. Mrs. Thomas came back in with a large bottle of shampoo and proceeded to wash their hair, not once but half a dozen times. The shampoo was all used up and the bathwater had to be changed several times. When their mother started attacking their black necks with a scrubbing brush both boys thought they were being tortured.

After two hours of scrubbing and cleaning, Mrs. Thomas was fairly satisfied with her handywork. The boys were sore from the scrubbing, and although they were clean again, the smell of tar still lingered on their bodies. Even their father's deodorant spray couldn't mask it completely. Dressed in some clean clothes, their old ones had to be thrown away, they went downstairs to tell their parents of the events that led to them being covered in tar.

On hearing what they had done and how they saved Mrs. Muldoon's house, their parents' anger seemed to disappear, and the boys were pleasantly surprised when they were not given the telling off they expected. Mr. Thomas even said he would go to the party at Sleepy Hollow, as his wife was unable to attend.

At three o'clock the next day the guests had all assembled at Sleepy Hollow, Mrs. Muldoon, dressed in her best outfit, welcomed the guests and gave the adults a glass of sherry and the boys glasses of pop. There was even a photographer from a local newspaper to take their photographs.

"Where are the animals?" asked Ted.

"I thought it would be better if Louis and Samantha stayed in the cellar for now." Mrs. Muldoon told him. "Ponsonby and Dilys are in the kitchen."

"Did you find Henry and Henrietta?" asked Peter, referring to the missing hedgehogs.

"No, I'm afraid they are gone for good." said Mrs. Muldoon sadly.

"They'll turn up." said Paul reassuringly.

"This is no time to be sad." announced Mrs. Muldoon and turned to speak to her guests. She raised her glass.

"I give you a toast." she told them. "To Ted, Paul, and Peter and the Battle for Sleepy Hollow."

"To Ted, Paul, and Peter and the Battle for Sleepy Hollow." repeated the guests, raising their glasses to the boys.

Even Mr. James joined in the toast and the photographer took another photograph.

"Please be seated." Mrs. Muldoon told her guests.

Everyone sat down, but Mr. James was on his feet again with a yell of pain.

"Whatever is the matter?" asked a concerned

Mrs. Muldoon.
"I've been stabbed in the bottom." wailed the unfortunate Deputy Clerk.

Mrs. Muldoon went over to his chair.

"Oh Mr. James." she shouted, hugging him.
"You've found Henry and Henrietta."
"I think they found him." laughed Ted.

Just then Ted felt something licking the back of his neck. He turned around to find Dilys giving him a kiss.

"Cut it out Dilys." objected Ted.

Dilys went over to Paul and Peter giving them a lick in turn.

"She's showing that she likes you." explained Mrs. Muldoon.
"It's not that." said Ted. "She's showing us she likes the smell of us."
"What do you mean?" asked his father.
"It's the smell of that liquid." explained Ted. "She can still smell it on us."

The guests burst into fits of laughter.

"Hee-haw, hee-haw, hee-haw." brayed Dilys, joining in the laughter in her own way.

The following week the boys' photograph appeared in the local newspaper with an account of their adventure. The gang had to make the boys members now as there was proof of their passing the test in the newspaper.

After the Easter holidays, when the boys returned to school, they had another pleasant surprise. Their teacher, Miss Hughes, was so impressed with what they had done that she decided to make the three boys' joint winners of the mystery prize for the best project done on the village during the holidays.

What was the mystery prize? Well, it wouldn't be a mystery prize if you knew what it was, would it?

THE END
B. K. Godwin
August 1976

A SNEAK PREVIEW OF THE NEXT BOOK.

Ted & Paul

Adventures with Cousin Clarissa

CHAPTER 1

BAD NEWS FOR THE BOYS

"Ted, Paul, will you get up! You'll be late for school."

Mrs. Thomas' voice rang up the stairs to her sons' bedroom. In the bedroom there was a grunting sound as Ted slowly emerged from under his pile of blankets. He gave a huge yawn.
"O.K Mam." he yelled back to his mother.

He quickly got out of bed and dressed hurriedly. There was no sign of his brother, just a big lump under the blankets on his brothers bed. Ted went to the bathroom for a quick wash. Ted would have earned an entry in the Guinness Book of Records for the fastest wash if there had been such an entry.
When he got back to the bedroom, the big lump was still under the blankets.

"Rise and shine." shouted Ted, pulling the bedclothes off his brother.
"Ugh!" grunted Paul and pulled them back over himself.
"Come on Paul." said Ted, pulling them off once

again. "If you don't get up, Mam will be up here after you."

"All right." grumbled his brother. "I'll be down in a minute."

"See you downstairs then." said Ted.

Ted rushed out of the bedroom, across the landing and thundered down the stairs and into the kitchen. His father was sitting at the table finishing his breakfast while his mother was preparing her husband's sandwiches for his lunch.

"Morning Mam, morning Dad." Ted greeted his parents.

"Do you have to come down the stairs like that?" snapped his father.

"Like what, Dad?" asked Ted.

"Like an elephant." shouted his father. "One of these days you'll go straight through them!"

"Sorry, Dad." apologised Ted.

He could see his father was in a bad mood this morning. Perhaps he had failed to win a fortune on the football pools yet again.

"Sit down and get your breakfast." his mother told him.

Ted sat down at the table next to his father and reached across the table for the packet of cornflakes. Unfortunately, his arm brushed against his father's cup of tea knocking it over, spilling the contents over the newspaper he was reading.

"You clumsy young idiot." yelled his father.
"Sorry Dad." mumbled Ted.
"It's all over the sports page." complained his father, "I can't read it like this."
"I'll dry it for you." said Ted, trying to be helpful.
"And how are you going to do that?" demanded his father.
"I'll put it in the oven for a couple of minutes." said Ted. "It'll soon dry in there."

Before he could stop him, Ted had taken the soggy newspaper off his father and put it into the oven. Mr. Thomas was just about to tell his son that it was a stupid thing to do as it might cause a fire when his wife distracted him by giving him another cup of tea. He stood by the kitchen door to drink it, well away from his son. There was a thundering sound across the landing and down the stairs.
"Look out." warned Mr. Thomas, "Here comes elephant number two."

Paul came charging into the kitchen pushing the door open right into his father who was standing next to it. The cup and saucer were knocked out of his hand and went sailing through the air.

"Oh look." said Ted, "A flying saucer."

The cup and saucer continued to sail through the air until gravity started to take effect. Crockery and tea crashed to the floor, the cup and saucer smashing and the tea splashing over Tibs the cat who was asleep in his basket. With a loud wail the cat fled from the kitchen.

"Gosh, I'm sorry Dad." apologised Paul.

Ted nearly choked on his cornflakes. Mr. Thomas glared at Paul and then at Ted. Paul expected his father to blow his top but he calmy went over to his wife and kissed her goodbye, "I'm going to work." he told her, "before our two sons do me an injury!"

"What's cooking, Mam?" asked Paul.
"Nothing." said his mother.
"That's funny." said Paul. "I can smell something burning and there's smoke coming out of the oven."

"My paper!" yelled Mr. Thomas rushing over to
the oven.

In the oven, the paper, or rather what was left of
it was fast becoming a pile of ashes. There was
nothing Mr. Thomas could do but let it burn. He
had been silly to let Ted put it in the oven, he
could have burned the house down. With a final
glare at his two sons, Mr. Thomas picked up his
briefcase and stormed out of the house,
slamming the door behind him.

"What's up with old misery guts?" Paul asked his
brother.
"Paul!" warned his mother. "Get your breakfast."
"But why did he put his newspaper in the oven?"
asked Paul.
"He didn't. I did." said Ted.
"Well that was a daft thing to do." said his brother.
"Why did you do it?"
"To dry it." explained Ted.
"How did it get wet?" asked Paul, "It's not raining
this morning."
"I tipped his cup of tea over it." giggled Ted.

Paul couldn't help laughing as well. No wonder
his father was in such a bad mood.
Their mother came and sat at the table with

them. She had a letter in her hand.

"I've had a letter." she announced.
"So we see." said Ted.
"Who's it from?" asked Paul.
"It's from your Aunty Gwyneth...." began his mother.
"Don't tell us she's coming to stay again." interrupted Ted.
"Ted!" scolded his mother. "That's no way to speak about your aunty."
"When is she coming?" groaned Ted.
"She is not coming." his mother told him.
"Thank goodness." said Ted with a sigh of relief.
"Ted, I won't warn you again." said his mother.
"Why has she written?" asked Paul.
"As I was saying," continued their mother, Aunty Gwyneth is not coming to stay but your cousin is."
"What!" yelled Ted jumping up.
"Not Clarissa the crab!" groaned Paul.

Comments from former pupils & residents of Cwmcarn village when they found out Ted and Paul stories were finally going to be published.

'I can't wait to share this book with my 4-year-old daughter. A piece of my childhood in hers.'
Rachael L Curran

'The thought of returning to stories that were the highlight of my school day is amazing. Being able to share them with my own daughter is just incredible.'
Jessica Jackson

'Awesome! Cannot wait to read them to my daughter.'
Nicola Jayne

'Brilliant news! Loved these stories at the end of the day after a hard days learning. Definitely will be purchasing. Nice one Mr. Godwin,'
Adam Carnell

'This has made my year! Can't wait for my children to read them.'
Becki Hodges

'This is amazing! I cannot wait for my daughter to read them. We always try singing her your songs you've made over the years that we can remember, so will be lovely to be able to read these to her.'
Emily Weetch

'Always remember my children telling me about your stories which they loved. Now our Grandchildren will have the pleasure of listening to them.'
Gaynor Badham

'Ted and Paul stories were the highlight of my school day. I remember everyone would behave really well in the afternoon so we could finish work early so we could listen to a few chapters. We would be gutted when the bell rang for home time.'
Emma Jean Hayes

'I used to love being immersed into the world of Ted and Paul. Mr. Godwin was such a brilliant storyteller and brought all of the characters to life. I can't wait to read these books.'
Eleanor Anne

'Mr. Godwin and his Ted and Paul stories were, as many other ex-pupils have said, the best part of being in his class / Cwmcarn Primary School. As a result of this book he has ensured that future generations of former pupils can enjoy his talent of writing. How can anyone not love Ted and Paul?'
Craig John

'Brilliant stories and used to look forward to these at the end of each day when I was in Mr. Godwin's class. (93/94). Also, if you were in Mrs. Hawkins class in 94/95 and you got into trouble during the afternoon you would be sent to Mr. Godwin's class for punishment, which if you timed it right would be just in time for Ted & Paul stories. Result!'
Nathan Kethro

'Amazing stories from an amazing teacher. Best time of the day was Ted and Paul time.'
Matthew Harris

'I loved the stories and remembered Mr. Godwin telling them. They deserve to be published for such an amazing person and teacher. We love Ted and Paul stories. Thank you for them.'
Lisa Illsley

'When the news broke, that Mr. Godwin was going to have his Ted and Paul stories published there was tangible excitement from all past pupils from way back when! Every pupil looked forward to story time in year 5, some of us were lucky enough to have 2 years with Mr. Godwin, so we had the pleasure of Ted and Paul twice over. Mr. Godwin was a favourite of so many pupils. You left and imprint in our hearts! Thank You Sir!'

Rebecca Watkins

'Mr. Godwin's storytelling during my formative years has left a warm and lasting impression well into my adulthood. How lovely that his work can now find a place in the hearts of others, and they can discover a little of what it was like to be his student.'

Robert Green

'What an amazing way to bring back memories of my childhood. The whole class were so excited when we saw the folder coming off the shelf and we would hear all about the adventures of Ted and Paul. Cannot wait to read them to my daughter.'

Lauren Watson

'It's pretty incredible that the stories Mr. Godwin told us as children will now be told to our children and grandchildren. what an incredible legacy from an incredible teacher.'
Stacey Brewster Hawdon

An inspirational teacher who made learning fun! I loved my school days at Cwmcarn (71-76). This has brought sunshine to a lot of people in these strange times! Thank you.
Jaki Southgate

I was a pupil of Mr. Godwin's from 88-89. I cannot put into words how happy this news made me. I remember my time in his class fondly and cannot wait to read these to my son.
Heidi Jeffries

'Absolutely beaming that Mr. Godwin is finally publishing his Ted and Paul stories. He was definitely the most wanted teacher for Year 5 & 6, and I was lucky enough to have him for 2 years! After a rough pandemic this was the news, we all needed. 100% my favourite teacher through all the years in education. '
Laura Weeks

Printed in Great Britain
by Amazon

63411565R00092